GOLD OF THE
RIO ESTRELLA

Stevens McClellan

Copyright © 2024 Stevens McClellan
All rights reserved
First Edition

PAGE PUBLISHING
Conneaut Lake, PA

First originally published by Page Publishing 2024

ISBN 979-8-89315-062-9 (pbk)
ISBN 979-8-89315-081-0 (digital)

Printed in the United States of America

Chapter 1

"I want a kid," she said, looking directly at Alec Jones. He looked at her for a moment.

"So you want to have sex?"

"Duh, no! You have to supply the sperm. I'll do the rest."

"Artificial insemination. That's a little difficult out here where we are, don't you think?"

"You get me the stuff, I'll do the rest," she said firmly.

He studied the fire for a while. At last, he sighed heavily and said, "No."

"Why not?" she asked.

"Well, for starters, it's my stuff. You have treated me like a persona non grata for the past two weeks. Ever since you completed your recovery from the crash. For you to demand favors from me, especially one so personal, is not only bizarre, it's completely unfair, despite our age differences."

She watched him for some time. The fire crackled, sending sparks flying high into the night sky. She tracked them until they burned out against the blanket of deep black. "Is this how you figure to get some sex from me?" she finally asked.

He looked at her, not really believing she had brought up this particular topic. "I wasn't figuring anything," he said. "You brought it up. If, however, you give this a little thought, you will have to concede that just keeping the two of us alive out here in this country is about all we are going to be able to accomplish."

"I'm thinking long-term," she said. "Here we are. You are about seventy-five. I'm twenty-seven. You aren't likely to last more than five to ten more years. If I have a kid now, by the time you kick it, the kid will be able to help me. His brothers and sisters will also contribute."

"Brothers and sisters?"

"Yeah. I want a kid a year for as long as you live."

"Well, you need to take another look. I'm forty-two, not seventy-five. And quite frankly, even if you had asked such a thing of me in a civil manner, I would have declined. You and I are not compatible in any way I can think of."

"This is survival. Not compatibility," she said. "Give it some thought, and you will see what I do. Without being rescued, we're on our own. The sooner we start procreating, the better."

"Well, start thinking about survival on your own because if that is your best plan for the future, I'll take my chances on surviving on my own till rescue comes, or I croak," he said stiffly.

Sensing a challenge, she rose to what she perceived as bait. Raising her voice, she attempted to dominate him. "So take your sorry ass and haul, then if that's all you can say," she shouted, "I don't need you for anything else."

"Okay," he said. "In the morning, we'll divvy up what we have, and I'll say so long."

"Good! I can't wait."

The night crawled by for both of them. The noises of the jungle were not as soothing as they had been prior to the present animosity. Their jangled nerves made for restless and interrupted sleep. Then at dawn, the yawps and howls of the red howler monkeys made things even worse as a troop moved through the canopy of the laurel and mahogany trees overhead.

The following morning, Alec sat Jordanne down and tried to make some sense of the previous evening's talk. She chose to remain obstinate, insisting that she could make it without his help. "Get out," she said over and over.

"Well," he finally gave up. "If you need help, or you want to try to set up housekeeping like a normal man and wife would, we can talk again. I'll stop by from time to time and see how you are doing."

"Don't bother," she said with more bravado than she really felt.

He sensed her bluff. He grinned and said, "Loco da vici."

As he swung the pack he had assembled from their worldly goods onto his back and set off through the brush and timber, she called, "What does that mean?'

"Oh, you'll see!" he yelled. "You'll see!"

Alec Jones was a touch over six feet in height. He kept himself in decent shape, although he wasn't fanatic about it. His shoulders were fairly broad. His legs were solidly muscled and strong. He had a full head of hair, dark brown shading to black. He wore it swept back and neat. His eyes were startling in that they were a dark smoky gray color that seemed to vary in color from smoke to almost black. Eyebrows, black and slightly arched, graced a solid brow. His face was chiseled with a straight jawline, tight chin, and high prominent cheekbones. His ears were of medium size and tucked neatly to the side of his head. At the moment, he was bearded with a two-week growth of dark-brown stubble, which promised to be a thick and full beard if not trimmed or shaved. Overall, he would be classified as passably good-looking, if not handsome.

As he bucked his way through the heavy cover, Alec reflected on the situation at hand. This stranded-in-the-wilderness event was not without precedent. Planes crashed all the time in back country places on most continents. The one he and Jordanne had survived just happened to be in a backward country on a developing continent. Rescue could take a while. Not as long as Jordanne was thinking, but a good long time, nevertheless.

It was a puzzle to him how some people survived where others didn't. The small plane the two of them were flying was occupied by the pilot, Jordanne, and her sister and brother-in-law, and himself. The trouble had begun about halfway through the three-hundred-mile trip. The engine had coughed, caught itself, smoothed out for a while, and then just quit. The pilot had done all the right things, broadcasting 'Mayday! Mayday!' and the coordinates for their location—the drainage of the Rio Estrella—and so on. The glide path for the crash was straight into heavy cover, the worst kind of stuff to spot a crash scene in. The plane had broken up like so many do; however, it did not burn. It simply skimmed along clipping treetops and slowing substantially until it struck a very large unforgiving tree. Everyone in the plane was hurled at sixty miles an hour into their seatbelts. Those in front were crunched into the compacted nose cowling and engine. Alec and Jordanne, seated in the back, were vee-jacked into the seatbacks in front of them. They were knocked unconscious but were the only survivors.

The plane had spun and then flopped on its side in a rather heavy brush. When Alec came to, he was gripped with a driving headache that nearly blinded him. Still, he had sensed that the plane was in danger of catching fire and exploding. He had scrambled loose from debris that had buried him completely. Running and thrashing downhill for a hundred yards had been agony, ending with him on his hands and knees, emptying his stomach. At that point, he had blacked out again.

After hours, he had regained his senses enough to assess the situation. Suspecting a severe concussion, he had slowly worked his way back to the plane. The bodies of the dead were strewn inside and out of what remained of the plane. It was then that he had discovered that Jordanne was still breathing. He had administered first aid to her, consisting of removing her from the fuselage and laying her on the ground with her legs elevated. He had suspected that she had the same concussion as himself, but she also had suffered a sharp blow to the ribs. At first, he feared internal injuries, but she did not cough up blood, so he had decided to leave her be, hoping that she would come around on her own.

He had examined the plane. It should have burned, he had figured, but since it had not, he had set about preserving as much of its gas and oil as he could. One wing tank had ruptured on the glide path to the crash and had dumped all its fuel. The other had miraculously been torn loose from the fuselage, along with its wing, and been deposited past the tree and into the hillside. It contained some of its fuel. He thought a few gallons anyway. He had only to use a rock to hammer shut its fuel line to the engine to preserve the contents. The crankcase had cracked and was dripping the last of its oil into the ground, but he had managed to find a container and had saved about a quart or so of oil.

Then he had dug through the pile of freight the plane had been carrying until he had found a shovel that Jordanne's mining engineer brother-in-law had packed aboard. It took a long time, until nearly dark, to dig a hole big enough to place the bodies of the dead within. He was exhausted beyond his own belief when he stumbled and crawled back to see how Jordanne was doing. There was no change. He had then scrounged through the wreckage until he had uncovered four bottles of water. He drank two and used one to bathe Jordanne's face and forehead. She remained unconscious. The fourth he saved.

The airplane's fuselage back of the wings had remained largely intact. Alec, from that point on, had begun to treat it as their roof. After shoveling aside enough detritus to drag, carry, and wool Jordanne into the aft portion of the tail section, he had settled down for the night. His view of the great mountains of South America, the Andes, looming out to the west, was stunning as their snow-clad peaks faded into the dark blue of creeping night.

The next morning brought no change to Jordanne's condition. He knew she had to have fluids, so he had held her upright and poured small amounts of water into her mouth. After losing most of the fourth bottle, she had started to make little sucking motions, which worked well enough to get a cupful or so of water into her stomach. He had then started the serious business of sorting the pile of debris into stuff they could use to survive.

His own concussion affected him in waves. Sometimes he would have to stop and rest for minutes at a time. Sometimes he had simply fallen into involuntary naps of a half hour or so.

A major find was a small carton of fire-starter materials, including a half dozen barbecue-style fire starters. He had also gotten lucky after three or four hours and had found the rest of the carton of water that had been stored onboard for the flight. He thanked the local government for requiring that at least one carton of water was packed aboard all small plane flights into the back country. He now had thirteen bottles of water, which he planned to hoard like gold. He had also found a how-to book on survival in the outback. It included edible plant as well as animal identification information.

With more confidence, he had administered an afternoon session of watering to Jordanne. She had taken to moaning painfully when he gave her the water to the point that the moaning interfered with her drinking. So he had decided to wrap her ribcage. Using clothing he had removed from the corpses, he had ripped some strips of cloth into long lengths he could overlap and use to bind her ribs. It was then that he had noticed, in a personal way, his campmate. She was tall, blonde, and trim in the shape of weekend warriors who run miles to stay shapely and attractive. To that end, she had done admirably well. Facially, she was striking. Her face had the classic olive shape that is universally recognized around the world as the basis to beauty. She had deep blue eyes, fringed with naturally long lashes, and eyebrows which were quite dark for a natural blonde. They were full throughout and were straight until two-thirds of the way where they broke sharply downward, forming an elongated L. Her legs were long and slender with well-defined musculature.

"I'm glad you are out cold," he had muttered to himself as he removed her blouse and bra and began wrapping her torso. He had a tough time getting the job done as his cinching the cloth bore through her unconsciousness enough for her to feel severe pain, causing her to thrash and resist his clumsy ministrations. Then he had replaced her blouse and begun the process of giving her water again. He wasn't sure how much she drank, but he quit after dribbling and spilling most of bottle number 3 into her mouth. The final slug, he drank himself.

Then had come the compelling task of rounding up food. The plane was his best source. He dug in like a badger. Everything he had found had a short shelf life. It became apparent that he would have to grub it out from the area around the plane for naturally occurring food. He was at almost totally loose ends in that department.

At first, Alec concentrated on affecting strategies to assist rescue. Smoky fire being his primary strategy, but he also maintained a sharp lookout for over flights by either fixed-wing aircraft or helicopter. None came.

What he didn't know was that a coup attempt against the local government had been launched almost simultaneously with their lift-off. It had failed, but in the turmoil, the record of their Mayday had been lost.

Chapter 2

Now, two weeks later, he had to deal with the idiot he had left at the plane. He accused himself of being an idiot for relinquishing his spot in the plane. His independence lasted three days and two torrential downpours. Still, he had his manly pride to consider, so he had stuck it out. Late in the evening of the third day, he stood before her as she crawled out of fuselage refuge. "What do you want?" she demanded.

"You hungry?"

"Yeah, so what?"

"Food," he said, tossing in front of her the fresh body of a snake he had killed and beheaded. "Here's my knife."

"Get a fire started," she demanded as she pounced upon the twisting body, pinning it with a leg while opening the clasp knife. She quickly began skinning the snake.

"There are conditions," he said.

"What conditions?"

"I am moving back into the plane."

"As long as you bring in food, I don't care. But I have a condition too."

"Don't tell me! That, again."

"Yep." She grinned.

He looked at her critically. "So what kind of delivery system have you come up with?"

"I can't find one as easy as the natural way, so we will do it that way. Don't expect me to enjoy it, however. You get to pile on for five minutes. No kissing. Just do it and get off."

"Rather mechanical, don't you think?"

"Yeah. Very. I like that thought. You will be my mechanic. Service the chassis and be done with it."

"Oh, brother," he said. "Like in a clinic. I can't wait for that experience."

"How's that fire coming?"

"Finished."

She had spitted two sections of the snake on sharpened sticks he had brought along with the snake. She handed one to him. Silently, the two of them concentrated for the next several minutes on roasting their meal. After they had eaten, Jordanne wiped her hands on her pants and stood up in front of Alec. "Well," she said, "let's get to it. The sooner we do it, the sooner we'll get a routine down."

"Come on, Jordanne, I can't do it just like that. Like animals. Worse than animals. We aren't even in heat!"

"So what! If that's what you want, you'll never get a piece. So come on. We'll make it quick."

With that, she shucked out of her pants and panties. Naked from the waist down, she crawled into the fuselage and lay down on her back. "Come on," she commanded, "get in here and get it over with."

"No," he said firmly. "I will not service you like a robot."

"What! I'm not pretty enough? Not built well enough for you? What is it?" she demanded.

"It's your pickup lines," he said. "You smooth-talking bitch, you."

"Don't you call me a bitch, you bastard!" she shouted.

"Then quit acting like one! And get your pants back on. You are wasting your time unless you are going on autopilot."

Angrily, she crawled out and redressed. "What is it going to take to get you to do your duty?"

He looked at her and smiled. "When it isn't a duty."

"Don't hold your breath on that!" she said, still hot and angry.

"I can do that, seeing as how I'm not missing much."

"You have no idea what you're missing, damn you!" she shouted.

"Then you better figure out how to show it, because right now, on a scale of 1 to 10, your needle has to go some to get to zero."

"If the ugliest man on Earth were here right now, I'd do him before you!"

"Good, that would be a relief."

"Bastard!"

"Bitch."

So their conversation ended, and they went to bed. A very strained relationship began, and a struggle of behemoth dimensions to survive was launched. Like it or not, deep down, the two knew they had to work together to make it.

The next morning, Alec awoke early and started a fire. He used fuel from the intact tank of the plane. His technique was to dribble fuel into one of the empty water bottles, cap it, and pour what he needed on his fire materiel when he was building a fire. It was a lazy way to start fires, but he had no desire to make fire starting more difficult. Despite the basically tropical latitude of the crash site of the plane, mornings began on the chilly side. He was cooking a piece of the snake left over from the previous evening. When he had scoured the debris field, he had recovered some salt and pepper. Now he sprinkled some of both on the spitted chunk of snake. The odor awakened Jordanne, and she crawled out of the fuselage. "Where's mine?" she demanded.

Alec nodded to the carcass dangling from the branch of a tree where they had stowed it. "Over there. Help yourself."

"Jesus! What a nice guy you are. Haven't you ever considered helping a lady?"

"Show me one, and I will."

"You just wait! I'll show you one," she said.

He looked at her before he spoke. He thought, *We need to bury the hatchet for the benefit of both of us.* So he pulled his punch and said more amiably than he felt, "I'm sure you can, given some time."

She stopped carving off a piece of the snake and glanced over her shoulder, sizing up his comment. "Yeah, well don't hold your breath on that. There is a major stumbling block to that."

"Let me guess. Me?"

"No shit, Sherlock! You figured that out all on your own. I am impressed."

"Have some salt and pepper."

"Where was this last night?"

"Last night, you were too bitchy."

"Ah-ha, I get it! You're trying to bribe me."

Alec looked at her, wanting to slap her impertinent face. "No, but if it helps us to work together so we can get out of here, so be it."

"Ain't that special!" she said, arching an eyebrow skeptically. "I can see what you really want."

"What would that be?"

"Hot sex!" she exclaimed triumphantly. "You want the good stuff! Well, I've already told you that you can have sex any time you want it, but it's going to be served cold, cold, cold."

"I don't want sex from you hot, cold, warm, icy, or any other way you can think of. Get that screwy idea out of your head. We are in a very dangerous situation here, Jordanne, and we need to work together. This could be life or death at any sudden moment. You need to get serious about what matters right now."

"Fine! Right after breakfast, you just point me in the right serious direction, and I'll get right to it."

Alec looked at her in disbelief. It had been his intention to explore for a route down off the ridge to the river that undoubtedly coursed through the canyon bottom below them. Taking her along had been in his mind, but her impudent attitude could be dangerous. Nonetheless, he decided to give it a try. "What I have in mind is to find a way down to the river. We need to find a reliable food source."

"Like what?" she interrupted.

"Fish."

"That sounds like your department. I've never caught a fish in my life."

"Before we get out of here, you're likely to do a lot of things you've never done in your life."

"So where's my pole?"

"It's down there. I have scavenged some stuff we can use for line and hooks, but we'll cut our fishing rods from the trees down at the water. We'll take a piece of the snake to use for bait."

"Okay. Bwana. Lead the way."

"I will, but first, we need to gear up."

With that, Alec laid out what he thought they could carry that would be helpful. He had saved belts and shoes, along with any useful articles of clothing from the dead before their burial. The same went for baggage from the wreck. Now he began setting out attire for Jordanne. As expected, she balked.

"Those are men's pants! Whose?" she demanded.

"I don't know. Yours now."

"Hey! I recognize those pants. You expect me to wear my dead brother-in-law's pants!"

"Yes. You will also wear this blouse over that hat, which was probably the pilot's."

"Why?"

"Bugs. Clouds of them. Biters, every damned one. Some will bore right through that blouse you're wearing. That's why you have to carry this jacket. It's denim. When we hit the swarms, you'll be damned glad you've got it. Same for the pants. Find a pair of shoes that will cover your ankles. Those flats you've been wearing won't cut it. Be sure to put on a pair of socks that will top your shoes."

"You're serious about this, aren't you?"

"I am, and you need to get serious too. By the time we get down to the river, we are going to have hiked, scrambled, and climbed three or four miles. It's not going to be easy, so we have to be as prepared as possible."

Jordanne looked off down the ridge to where the green mantle of the forest veed at the bottom of the drainage. "That's only about a mile down there. How do you get four miles out of that?"

"Because we're on foot. We can't fly down. I've already done a bit of exploration. There is a cliff that runs along parallel to the river. We have to work our way upstream toward the headwaters. The cliff isn't as high up there, and we should be able to climb down to the water. No promises, but it's our only shot."

"Well, I'm wearing those pants over mine. I can't stand the thought of Harry's pants next to my skin."

"I wouldn't advise that."

"Why?"

"Galls."

"What the hell are galls?"

"Rub marks that start as white blisters that sting like hell in your sweat and then burst into bloody marks that are worse. And in the worst place you can imagine."

"Like where? I don't want to imagine."

"Top of your legs in the creases of your ass and your dealy."

"Well, I'm not wearing Harry's pants!"

Alec looked at her in exasperation. "Okay. Here, you wear mine, and I'll wear his," he said, removing his trousers. "He and I were about the same size. In fact, he was a bit beefier. My pants will fit you better anyway."

"Well, aren't you the gallant one! Since you are out of your pants, how about it?"

"Later. Let's get going. Time's a wasting."

"That's a promise." She grinned at him.

"Promises are made to be broken," he said, pulling on Harry's pants. "Get those pants on and let's get out of here."

She finally settled down and dressed as he had advised. He then handed her a leather work glove and a machete he had recovered from the debris field of the crash. He retrieved the crude backpack he had made from a medium-sized piece of luggage and belts and straps. Into this, he had stuffed some cloth gloves he had scrounged, and the mate to the glove he had given Jordanne, along with the only canteen he had been able to find. To that, he included a pair of metal plates he had found from the strewn mess of the small kitchenette of the plane. He also added a pair of women's blouses. Fortunately, the two had been able to collect rainwater in a basin, like piece of the nose cowling of the plane. They had filled their plastic water bottles as often as it had rained. Water, he had discovered, was the one essential they had in abundance. He tucked in two water bottles apiece.

"So what did you say you want me to do with this knife thing?" she asked as they set out.

"Whack the brush and trees ever so often so we have sign we can follow coming back. Here, hand me the machete, and I'll show you." She handed him the machete, and he clipped a brush branch off at waist height. A little further ahead, he chopped a blaze in a medium-sized tree.

"What's the glove for?"

"Blisters. After you've blazed a bunch of trees, you'll thank me."

"Why do I have to chop first?"

"Practice. When we get back here, finding the plane won't be too much of a problem, even in the dark. But we need to be sure we can find 'here.' Getting you used to how to blaze a trail is best done here. Then you'll be an old pro up there where it really counts."

Somewhat alarmed, she blurted, "In the dark? Aren't we coming back before dark?"

"I hope so. But let's make a good trail just in case."

He grinned to himself as he heard her whacking away behind him. Her vigor was the first positive thing she had done on her own for a long time. He was hopeful that she was turning a corner.

For several hours, they bushwhacked along the ridge, working higher and higher up the drainage. Several times they had to detour up small side drainages where streams that were too big and swift to cross poured down the ridge side on their way to the river below. In every case, the streams had cascaded into waterfalls over the massive cliff that bordered the river. Several times they had disturbed troops of monkeys that raced away overhead, screaming their protests. Alec had looked carefully at these small tributaries for signs of fish, frogs, salamanders, water crabs, snakes, and anything else that might constitute a food source. The only thing he found, growing at the water's edge, was a sort of tree spinach that he thought might be edible. He stuffed some in his backpack. He would look it up in his survival book when they returned to camp.

At last, they reached the river. The water where they struck it was a cascade. Alec found what appeared to be a small game trail that led downstream. The two followed it for a mile or so. Pools began forming as the flow of the river slowed. The bank began to get boggy in places. There, the trail turned into the trees to skirt those areas.

The bugs began to manifest themselves. The hikers paused and dressed their hats with the blouses Alec had packed. He also cut a pair of poles and rigged up fishing line and his improvised hooks. They donned the cloth gloves. He baited his with snake meat and began dapping, intending to show Jordanne the technique. She, however, had drifted away. He looked for her and found she had removed her boots and socks, rolled up her pants legs, and was wading at the edge of the pool.

Annoyed, he called to her, "Hey! What are you doing? You're scaring the fish away."

"Is this gold?" she asked, holding up a nugget between her thumb and fore finger.

"What? Let me see that," he said, striding quickly to her. She handed her find to him. He looked at it closely and noted its color and lack of crystalline structure. "Well," he said, "it's not iron pyrite. Yeah, you found a very nice piece of gold. Where did you find it?"

"In the gravel of that sandbar back there," she answered, pointing up stream to the structure ten yards away.

"Let's take a look," Alec said.

For the next fifteen minutes or so, the two of them tore into the little sand and gravel bar. They rooted with sticks they had picked up on the bank. They could see the yellow color rolling off the points of their sticks, but they ignored that as they were picking an astounding number of gold nuggets just using their hands. Alec was beside himself. "Jesus Christ!" he exclaimed. "We fly into this godforsaken place, crash, and find the gold that your brother-in-law couldn't find in his diggings a 150 miles from here. I don't know if we can keep it in this godforsaken backwater, but this stream is a placer miner's dream come true!"

"So you're saying I did good?"

"No, I'm saying you did fantastic, girl! This is an Eldorado."

Jordanne found herself inwardly pitching in with him. "So what are we going to do about it?" she asked eagerly.

Alec was counting their pickers. In size, they ranged from that of a small pea to an apricot pit. There were seventeen of them. "Kid, we are going to go fishing and think about this" was his answer. He walked to his backpack and stuffed the gold into it. "Follow me." He picked up their fishing gear and headed downstream to the next pool.

He added bait to her pole and showed her how to dap. The two of them fished the hole for half an hour, pulling out a half dozen heavy-bodied fish that looked very much like a species of trout. They were deep in the body with wide shoulders, and they averaged fourteen to eighteen inches in length. Alec called it off and added, "We have shore lunch."

He carried one of the fire starters with him at all times, so it didn't take him long to kick together a small fire in a little clearing back in the woods. To keep the bugs at bay, he occasionally tossed in a green branch for smoke. Using the metal plates from the backpack, he fried each of them three fish in their own plate. He had thoughtfully included his salt and pepper. As they ate, a sort of communal togetherness began to form with them. She praised his skill in locating a way to the river and finding the food source they badly needed. He gave her full credit for being curious enough to pick up their first gold nugget.

They had an adult conversation for once. She asked why they were nearly always awakened by the whoops and hollers of those red monkeys that traveled overhead. "I think the plane crashed in a travel way for that particular troop as it moves from food to water and back. They're probably pissed at us for disturbing their routine, so they let us know it. I imagine them saying to one another, 'So what's so special about those assholes? They can't even figure out how to feed themselves.'"

She laughed. "I hadn't thought of that, but I guess they have a point."

After they had polished off their fish meal, he said, "Let's use these fish guts and catch some more to take back to camp."

She was all in. "That's more fun than I thought. I don't even mind knocking them in the head and pulling their guts out."

"You are getting to be good at this. I think you caught the biggest one too. Let's see who can catch the biggest one this time."

For the next hour, they fished vigorously, but as happens with fishing, the bite was off. They fished two additional pools downstream. Alec tried fishing the water races between the pools, but the current was too swift for dapping. Between them, they caught four from the lower pools. Alec caught the biggest one but had to admit it was smaller than the big one Jordanne had caught earlier. The average was about the same as the first session. They each caught two. Alec cleaned his and Jordanne cleaned hers. He wrapped them in moss and placed them in his backpack. "Now what?" she asked. "Are we going to see if we can find some more gold?"

"No," he said. "We are gonna have to hustle to make it back to camp by dark. We'll come back with some equipment next time and take a better look. I really think you found a bonanza."

They made it back to the plane a little before dark. Alec looked up the plant he had found in his survival book. It was edible, and there were instructions on how to prepare it. Neither really liked it that well, but by salting it and taking out the center vein of the leaves, they both were able to tolerate it by eating it with fish. They saved two of their catch for the next day. They washed the meal down with water, and shortly after, they crawled into their fuselage shelter and stretched out on their sleeping pallets.

"So what do you think about today?" she asked sleepily.

"You'll do," he said. "You'll do."

Chapter 3

The next morning, Alec was sprung from slumber by a wild shriek that jerked him upright, causing him to crack his head on the roof of the fuselage. "What's going on!" he shouted in alarm, fearing a snake had crawled in with them.

"Get your hand off my ass!" Jordanne bellowed.

"It is off!" he exclaimed. "What was your ass doing where my hand could get to it anyway? You were behind me all night."

"I rolled over against something in the night. I wasn't even aware it was you. I didn't wake up."

"So you spooned me all night and are pissed off by my hand resting on your ass? What's wrong with you? Mother of God! Would you give me a break? Yesterday, we had a positive day. The first one we've had since we got here. And now you are off the deep end, again! For Chrit's sakes, Jordanne!"

She was stunned by the vehemence of his outburst. Lamely, she said, "I guess I overreacted. It just scared me is all. I agree, yesterday was great. I liked it a lot. This is my bad. It won't happen again."

"Well, I'd really like to believe you, but just saying it isn't proving anything." With that, he turned his attention to building up the fire and preparing their last two fish for breakfast.

They ate silently. When they were finished, Alec stated a plan for the day. "We could use some of the stuff that was on that plane that is out in the debris field. Searching that mess is going to be a bitch, but we need to do it."

She looked at him and nodded. "Okay," she said. "What are we looking for?"

"Cooking utensils for one. A decent pot or two, or something that would serve the same purpose. God, having a fork would be a blessing! A cooking pot for making stew would be nice. Or even something like that, that could serve the purpose. There was a rifle with ammunition. I saw it. If we could find it, that would be terrific for the short-term. Look for anything that we can repurpose. Rescue, for whatever reason, is not happening for us. We have to get serious about survival. Long-term survival."

They spent the day working a grid. Alec used the shovel, turning over anything that looked promising and digging up whatever was partially buried. Among their discoveries was the rifle. It contained four cartridges in the magazine. Alec determined that he would keep searching for the box of ammo. Jordanne had found the bulk of the kitchenette. There was a mid-sized pot, crushed, two spoons, a table knife, a pair of kitchen knives, and two forks. Alec found the stainless-steel sink from the compact restroom. He also unearthed some of the mining supplies that were on board. A badly damaged gold pan, a small pickaxe, minus the handle, and some rope that had been ground into the forest floor. He pulled and worked it with the shovel until he had recovered in three different lengths, around seventy-five feet. Additionally, they had compiled miscellaneous other bits and pieces of metal. The final find was the head of a fire axe that was either a stowaway aboard the plane, or part of the mining equipment. Both found various articles of clothing that had been strewn and half buried.

Altogether, they were pleased with their booty. They had both gotten grimy from head to foot. "I wish I had found some soap," Jordanne mentioned as they sat thinking of repurposing their stuff.

Alec looked at her, grinned, and pulled a bar of soap, still in its wrapper, from his pocket. He flipped it to her and looked up into a darkening sky. "Your shower, milady," he said, "is coming right up. I will be refilling our water bottles." He moved a discreet distance away and, using the sink, positioned a water bottle under a short pipe stub still attached to the sink drain. Soon, the storm descended upon them. Alec stripped down to his underwear and rinsed off as best he could while using the crude stand he had previously put together when he had collected water in the piece of cowling. Once, he glanced behind him. He was checking to see how Jordanne was doing. He was startled to see her leaning over naked with her back to him as she rinsed out her hair. He immediately spun back around, but the picture was imprinted. He could not unsee it. He studiously worked on his task until he was sure she had finished. He redressed and returned to the fuselage.

"Get 'em all filled up?" she asked.

"Got 'em," he said.

"Did you fill up anything else?"

"I wasn't trying to look at you, or anything," he said, feeling guilty. "Besides, it's not as if I haven't seen it before."

"Not like that though, huh?"

"No, not like that."

"So what do you think?"

"Well, I don't think."

"Liar, liar, pants on fire!"

"Oh, for God's sake! Let's find something else to talk about."

"You can put your hand on my ass if you want."

"Y-y-you are unbelievable," he stuttered.

"I try." She smiled. "And I probably won't stop. So reset. Get used to it. By the way, those galls you were talking about? They're for real. I'm getting rid of my bra. But I'll keep it so we can tote stuff in the cups!"

He turned away. "Good God, whatever that means," he muttered.

The following day, they returned to the river. The trek was quicker because they knew the trail and had blazed it out pretty well. They added additional blazing to improve the sight lines. Alec had added the gold pan which he had worked over until he was pretty sure it would function reasonably well. They went fishing first, using the fish guts from two days previously. Nothing was biting. Alec was getting more and more anxious and impatient as time wore on. Jordanne acted nonchalant, not really caring too much. To her, either there were fish that cooperated, or there weren't. She wasn't about to get frustrated about it.

At length, she sat down on a log near the edge of the water. Alec worked his way to her. "Give up?" he asked.

"No. Just wondering," she said.

"About what?"

"What else do fish eat besides two-day old rotten fish guts?"

"Insects, worms, hellgrammites, and other shit. I don't know what all. Why?"

"Why don't we try some of that?"

He stared at her. "Where do we get some of that?"

"You have that shovel. Don't worms live in the ground?"

"Oh my god, Alec!" he exclaimed, annoyed with himself. "Quit being so damned stupid."

In moments, he had set to with the shovel in a damp area next to the river. He turned over fat, beautiful, and lively worms with every turn of the spade. "Here," he said, happily handing her half a dozen, "let's get to fishing!"

Within twenty minutes, they had hauled out a dozen fish. After dressing them and lunching on four of them, they stowed away the rest in the backpack. Then Alec began working sand and gravel bars with the shovel and gold pan. Jordanne strolled around looking for nuggets. He was amazed at how much gold he was able to pan. He swirled each pan down until all the sand and fine gravel was thoroughly washed away. Then, using a foot-square piece of cloth, he dumped the collected gold into the middle of the cloth. Then he shook the gold into the bottom of his pack, which he had lined with the back of a shirt. The system, while a bit clumsy, was still an efficient way to capture nearly all that he panned. After an hour and a half, he took a break. He peered into the backpack to check his take. The gold glowed in a satisfactory layer an inch or two deep. Looking around, he saw that Jordanne had disappeared. He figured she had simply wandered down around a bend in the stream a quarter mile below where he was panning, so he returned to his task.

After a half hour, he began to get nervous about her absence, so he took another break and set out to search for her. As an afterthought, he grabbed the machete and took it with him. Rounding the bend of the river, he was astounded at a scene taking place on a sandbar. Jordanne was struggling with something. She would rise to her feet or knees, only to be thrown down and rolled around in a mass of dark-green coils. Alec sprinted the last hundred yards. Arriving on scene, he immediately saw that she was in dire straits. A snake, an anaconda, had her gripped in its jaws just below her left knee. It had encircled her waist and was working to get another coil about her head and shoulders. She had the snake's tail in both hands and was trying to keep her head free. She was screaming in terror, but no sound escaped her lips. The snake threw her again as Alec braced his legs. Her left leg cleared enough that he saw an opening and swung the machete with both hands. He hit the anaconda's neck about four inches behind its head. The snake went into a paroxysm of frantic motion. Its tail straightened out, giving Jordanne the advantage of squirming out of the second coil. Alec danced around the pile of flailing woman and snake. The blow he had delivered to the snake had cut deeply but had not severed the head completely. The snake held its grip and continued to strain mightily with its first coil. Alec found another opening and crashed the machete into the bloody cut behind the snake's head. That blow sliced the body free. It continued to writhe and twist powerfully, sweeping Jordanne around in the sand, but it had stopped constricting. Alec dropped the machete and sprang into the roiling mass. He had the bloody body below the severed head gripped tightly in both hands. Blood sprayed wildly over both of them, but he doggedly worked, jerking free the coil around her waist. It took a minute or more to pry the heavy coil loose enough that she could roll away from it. He then dragged the still struggling and coiling snake body away, far enough that it was no longer a danger to either of them.

    She was clearly in a state of shock and lay mute, staring at him uncomprehendingly. He ignored that and retrieved the machete. The head was still attached to her leg, and that was what demanded his immediate attention. He straddled her thigh and grabbed the head in his right hand on top and his left on the bottom. He couldn't loosen the grip. Next, he tried wedging the machete into the snake's mouth, but soon realized that that would cause severe injury to Jordanne. He sat back and looked around. He spotted a root ball from a fallen tree at the edge of the water just downstream. He grabbed the machete and ran to the root ball. He hacked several foot long chunks of root loose and ran back to where she was sitting up, looking at her leg.

"Just hang on," he said. "This is going to hurt."

He found that the snake had a lip flap that he could get a good grip on. He also saw that the snake's teeth curved backward like dozens of fishhooks. He grabbed the lip of the upper jaw in both hands and pulled up and forward with all the strength he could muster. The mouth gaped enough that he could force one of the root lengths under the teeth on the left side. He then repeated the process on the opposite side. Still, the head held on. "Roll over on your stomach," he commanded. She didn't move. "Jordanne, goddamnit!" he shouted at her. "Roll over on your stomach." Slowly, clearly suffering from shock, she turned over. He went to work on the bottom jaw of the snake. He quickly jerked the jaw up and forward. He crammed a root into the opening he had produced on the left. Then he rammed a longer piece through the open maw on the right. Grabbing that piece of root in both hands, he pulled the bottom jaw free of her leg. He rolled her away from him prying the head and its upper jaw off her leg. In the process, many of the teeth broke off and bristled in the bloody half oval prints in her flesh.

Exhausted, he pulled her to him. Together, they rocked back and forth. He held her and whispered to her that she would be all right. It was then that he realized how much he had feared for her life during the struggle. He was suffering from shock himself. He vowed to protect and take care of her. A half hour later, they were calm enough to assess the wound to her leg. She had finally regained her voice. "It's not hurting right now," she said. "See if you can pull them out."

Using his clasp knife, he soon had a system going. He would squeeze her skin with his left hand to protrude a tooth, and then with his right thumb and the blade of the knife, he would pluck the tooth out and toss it aside. In fifteen minutes, he had completed the task.

"Now what?" she asked.

"We need to clean those teeth punctures and wash off this blood," he said. "Come on." He took her hand gently and led her into the stream where the water was deep enough to cover her wounds.

"We're going to stand here for a while, so just lean against me. I won't let you fall."

He did the scrubbing of both of them. After what seemed like an hour, but was really about half that, he led her out of the water. "Do you remember where the first aid kit was stowed in the plane?" he asked her.

She looked at him as though he weren't there. "Was…was there one?" she finally stammered.

"Yes, honey, there was. Do you remember where it was?"

"I remember a white box behind the pilot's seat. Why?"

"I am going to find it if I have to dig that whole mountainside up. There will be stuff in it that will be critical to taking care of those bites. Now do you think you can travel?"

She nodded and suddenly said brightly, "But what about my snake?"

Vastly relieved at her outburst, he pulled her to him. She tilted her head, and he kissed her tenderly. She returned the kiss. They embraced for several seconds, both momentarily enchanted. "Don't worry about your snake," he said. "I'll get you another one."

Then moving as best they could, they gathered their stuff and headed back up the mountain. It was dark and late when they finally arrived at the fuselage. Neither of them in their bone-weary state felt like eating. They each drank a bottle of water and rolled into their beds. He cuddled her closely and worried for a long time before her even breathing soothed him to sleep.

Chapter 4

In the morning, Alec woke up first and crawled out without stirring Jordanne from an exhaustion-induced slumber. He assessed the sky for weather and was pleased to be greeted by a clear blue cloudless sky. Gratified for the prospect of good weather for at least the morning, he checked her forehead and face for signs of fever. She was lying on her stomach, which gave him the chance to examine her wounds. They were red and beginning to fester.

He looked over their collection of cloth articles and found a hand towel. He started a fire, and using the pot they had found and pried back into a usable shape, he heated water. Then he used the bar of soap to wash and rinse the cloth as clean as he could. When he finished, he watched Jordanne until she awakened. "How do you feel?" he asked.

"Like I pulled a train. Damn, that looks ugly enough," she said, peering and poking at the angry-looking bite marks.

"Don't touch!" he said quickly. "We want to keep infection to a minimum."

"Yeah, you're right. How are we gonna do that?"

"I'm going to find that first aid kit. If it's intact, it should have alcohol, hydrogen peroxide, aspirin, and gauze wraps and pads. And hopefully, a first aid manual."

"What am I going to do?"

"You are staying right here. I've washed out that hand towel. You need to keep it soaked in cool water and use it as a compress on your injury. If you start feeling feverish, you need to use it to bathe your face, forehead, back of your neck, and the undersides of your wrists. That's important to keep fever under control."

"Wow! Do you think I ought to bathe the insides of my thighs too?"

"No, I don't think…" he started and stopped. "Oh, come on! I'm being serious here."

"Speaking of," she smiled, "how serious were you last night?"

He looked away, studying the other side of the mountain. "Look," he said, "I probably took advantage of a vulnerable situation. Maybe we should just let that slide. I don't want you to get the wrong idea."

"Oh, I don't think I got the wrong idea. You keep saying we're in this together. You can't imagine how thankful I am that we were together last night after what we went through with that snake. So don't go 'Aw shucks' now, honey!"

"Aw, man, you don't forget anything, do you?"

"Nope. And don't forget, you owe me a snake."

"Are you hungry?" he asked her suddenly, changing the subject.

"Well, yes, sweetheart, I am! I'm so hungry I could eat a snake. A big one!"

"Brother," he groaned, "how the hell do I get into these situations?"

He bent to the task of preparing another feed of fish. They ate quietly, giving the banter a break.

When finished, she took their plates and forks. "I'll do the dishes!" she said.

He laughed and said, "Why, thank you, honey!"

They both laughed, and then suddenly kissed each other like a couple parting before going to work.

It was so spontaneous neither knew what to make of it. She broke the moment. "I like this new us."

"Yeah," he agreed. "The new us."

He searched the debris field in ever widening arcs for several hours. Back and forth, he worked the area to no avail. Then he took a break and examined how the plane had spun in. On a hunch, figuring that something as heavy as a metal case stocked full of medical supplies would carry a long way in a crash like the one the two of them had experienced, he went exploring beyond the obvious finish of the debris zone. He looked at how high the plane struck the last tree. He triangulated in his mind the trajectory such an object could take if it were flung free. He looked at the trees, along the imaginary path he had in mind.

Slowly, he walked the line. He finally noted a small broken branch about forty feet up in a mahogany tree. He looked back at the plane strike and lined that up with the branch. The drop was about fifty feet. Using that as a line, he searched the area forward of the branch. He found nothing on the ground. Then he looked up from a different angle, calculating the possible flight of the object that might have broken the branch. Twenty feet up, wedged in the crotch of a big limb and the trunk of a tree, he spotted a bit of white that was clearly out of place and mostly obscured by a ball of vines. Excited, he walked around the tree, staring up and trying to determine what the object was. Finally, he was convinced it was the first aid kit.

His next task was to get to the kit. The first level of branches was ten feet up. Strangler figs encircled the tree and crawled well up beyond where the kit was wedged in the crotch of the limb and trunk. The entire mass was richly imbedded with a vicious-looking thorn. Alec decided to go back to camp for equipment to tackle his climb up to the prize. He drove his shovel into the forest floor to mark the spot.

Upon his return to camp, he found Jordanne sitting in the shade, bathing her face with a soaking wet cloth. He knew immediately that fever had set in. He touched the back of his hand to her cheek. "Oh, Jesus!" he said. "You are definitely starting to fever up."

"I'm trying all the stuff you said, plus some," she said. "Did you find the thing?"

"I did, but it's wedged in a tree twenty feet up in a tangle of vines with four-inch thorns. I've got to figure out how to get up there. Any ideas?"

"Fly," she said.

"Well, my dear," he said, "you haven't lost your sense of humor. But seriously, we need to brainstorm this thing."

They discussed several ideas, including the wild idea of chopping the tree down. They finally decided that the best strategy was for him to pad up with extra pants and the leather gloves. He would use the machete on his way up, clipping off the thorns while using the vines as a ladder. She insisted upon going with him. Secretly, he was glad she did. She carried a length of rope just in case it could be used.

The vine was a strangler fig that encircled the entire trunk of the tree. They stood, looking up at the kit. They then walked the circumference, looking for the best place to tackle the task. There was no best spot. Alec picked a spot and started by using the machete to clip off thorns as high up as he could reach. Jordanne came up with the idea of using the rope to tie in stirrups as he moved up. That worked. She used his clasp knife to cut the lengths and tossed them to him as needed. He had tied a length of rope to the machete and to his belt, allowing him to use both hands to knot in the stirrup loops. By standing in the stirrups, he tied in as he moved up, holding on with his left hand, and swinging the machete with his right, he was able to work his way, clipping off thorns up to the crotch holding the kit.

It took a while to hack around the kit, but he finally worked it free. He turned around to look down and call to Jordanne to see if there was enough rope left to lower the kit to the ground. She reached up from where she stood in the stirrup, just below him, and handed him the rope.

"Goddamnit, Jordanne!" he yelled. "What are you doing!"

"Quit yelling at me! I'm helping!"

"What if you fell, for God's sake?"

"What if you did? I just have a fever. I'm not helpless. Quit coddling me, goddamnit it!"

"Oh, all right," he growled. "This is not the place to argue."

He passed the end of the rope through the handle of the first aid kit, tied it off, and lowered it to the ground. Then he followed her down. They left the stirrups in the tree. They didn't open the kit. On the way back, he carried the rope coiled up over his shoulder, plus the first aid kit. She carried the machete and shovel. Neither spoke. As they climbed the slight rise leading up to the tree of the crash strike, Alec kicked something in the ankle high brush, nearly felling him. "What was that?" he asked turning around to have a look.

"It's a box," she said. "Hey, it's the ammo you were looking for." She held it up for him to see.

"Oh my god!" he shouted. "This is a great day to be alive!" His joy broke their sullen silence.

She laughed. "I know! Believe me, I really know."

The first aid kit proved to be a godsend. None of its glass containers, due to the tight packing of the kit, were broken. It contained everything Alec had hoped for. He immediately began ministering to Jordanne. He gave her aspirin, and he used gauze pads and alcohol to sterilize the bite wounds on her leg. Then he carefully poured hydrogen peroxide into each tooth puncture as he pressed them open.

"Jesus!" she burst out. "Aren't you about done? That hurts like hell. And what's that fizzing noise?"

"No, I'm not done. This is what you get for climbing that damned tree and scaring the crap out of me! The fizz is the peroxide reacting to the pus in your bites."

"Pus?"

"Yes, pus. Your bites are starting to infect."

"What are you going to do about that?"

"When I'm done here," he said, "I'm going to read about it."

"What do you have left to do?"

"Iodine. It's going to sting."

Using the glass applicator rod, he worked iodine into each of the punctures. When he was finished, he reached up and slapped her butt. "There," he said. "All done."

She rolled over and sat up. "Aren't you gonna bandage it?" she asked.

"Only at night. It will heal faster in the open air. We have to keep flies away from it, though. We don't want to have to deal with maggots."

"Maggots?" she exclaimed.

"Yes. Flies will lay eggs in the wounds. The maggots will actually clean the rot, if it comes to that. Climbers who suffer severe frost bite in the high Himalayas and other mountains above about twenty thousand feet have actually benefited from maggot infestation in their dead skin caused by frost bite." He grinned at her and added, "But you won't get frost bite. I'll leach you before we try maggots."

"What do you mean, 'leach me'?"

"I'll go down to the river, find some leaches, bring them back, and attach them to your bites. They suck out the dead blood."

"Oh my god! You need to start reading," she said. "Right now!"

Alec leafed through the manual, finally coming to snake bites. Most of the material dealt with venomous bites. The part dealing with nonvenomous bites advised washing the bites with warm soap and water, going to your doctor for the removal of any teeth, and getting a tetanus shot. He looked up at her and said, "Just call me Dr. Jones."

"What?"

"Here, read this."

She frowned and said, "Son of a bitch! I'm being treated by a quack."

"At your service," he said, sweeping an arm before him.

"I'd pray if I was religious," she groused. "Are you?"

"Well, I believe in the Almighty, but I'm not much of a churchgoer."

"Good enough. We'll have prayers sessions several times a day. You should also pray privately, aloud preferably, so I know you are keeping the channel open."

"Har, har, har!" he returned with another grin. "I'll be sure to do that as I stick the leaches on your leg."

The following several days, Alec attended her, carefully monitoring for infection, keeping track of the progress of her fever, and watching for any fly infestation. That gave them time to fill in the gaps in their biographies. He asked her where she was from. "If I said I was from Swandip, Alberta, Canada, what would you say?"

"Bullshit."

"Let me guess where you're from: Limpdick, Nebraska."

"That's another bullshit."

"Well," she said, drawing it out, "you could have fooled me."

"What's your last name, by the way?" he asked.

"Guess."

"Easy."

"Ha ha," she smirked. "Austin."

"From where?"

"Actually, Phoenix, Arizona. Where are you from?"

"Well, it might as well be Limpdick. I'm from Omaha."

And so it went for nearly a week. She learned he was a quality and safety specialist for mining equipment, which explained why he was on the plane. He found that she was a physical fitness instructor on vacation with her sister and brother-in-law.

The team "New Us" buried the hatchet completely. Despite all that, they did not have sex. They slept side by side and spent much of their time simply enjoying each other's company. He trekked three times alone to the river and brought back fish each time. He also continued his harvest of the tree spinach. At the end of the week, she implored him for something besides fish. So he loaded the rifle and set out on the hunt. He was hoping for something in the line of red meat. "Will a monkey do?" he asked.

"Sure," she said. "Several of those damned howlers. Just plan on eating them yourself. Bring me something special, like a big rat."

He had to settle for a bird. He thought that, perhaps, it was a brush turkey. Whatever it was, the change was enormously popular with both of them.

Chapter 5

Jordanne's snake bites had closed quite nicely, and she was back on her feet. The two of them hiked down to the river. She was eager to look at the site of the snake fight. "Why?" he asked.

"I want to see if the gold I found is there."

"Oh, yeah. I suppose so," he said. Strangely, since the snake encounter, he had not thought about panning for more gold. He walked with her to the sand and gravel bar. They both looked first for the remains of the snake. It was gone. Alec looked for signs of the disappearance. He found tracks of animals, including the pug marks of a large cat. "Look at this," he said.

"Damn," she said, "are those cat tracks?"

"Yeah. Fresh too. No more than a day old. That means it won't be too far from here. We need to get out of here."

"Let me take a quick look for my gold."

"All right, but hurry. I'll keep watch."

She strode quickly to the fight scene. In a few minutes, she had recovered most of the gold she had found. "That's enough," he called. "We can get more later. Come on, let's get out of here!"

"We still need fish," she said. "You watch, and I'll catch. Shouldn't take long, but I'll need some worms. Let's fish that upper pool by the trail. We haven't hit it in quite a while."

"Yeah, you're right. When we get back, there's something I want to talk about with you."

As soon as they returned to the upper pool, he began digging for worms. "What do you want to talk about?"

"Later," he said, "when we have more time. Here you go. Get started while I dig some more."

He worked the shovel, and she fished and wondered what was on his mind. But unlike before, when they treated and spoke to each other sarcastically, she chose to bide her time. In a half hour, she had pulled out eight fish, typical of the size they had caught before. They quickly dressed them, wrapped them in moss, and stuffed them into the backpack. Alec had kept his head on a swivel for the entire time. On the way back, he trailed Jordanne and kept watching their back trail. He also paused long enough to harvest and stuff more of the tree spinach into the backpack. Their return was finished without incident.

After another fish dinner, they prepared for bed. He drew the rifle in with him. It didn't take her long to broach the subject of his secret. "Spill your guts!" she demanded.

He turned over on his side, where he could face her. "Okay. We are clearly not being looked for, that's number 1. We are lost somewhere in an unpopulated highland, that's number 2. The food we are eating is not going to keep us going, long-term, that's number 3. We now have a jaguar, I believe that's what made those pug marks, moving around in the area, that's number 4. The river will lead us out of here, that's number 5. We are going to run out of fire starter, that's number 5 1/2. And the gas tank for the fires is just about empty, that's number 6. I think we need to leave. What do you think?"

"Well, since we also aren't making a kid, that's number 7. So I say, why not leave?"

"Good!" he said. "By the way, is it still my duty?"

She smiled and rapidly batted her eyes at him. "No, it isn't, and the kitchen is getting warmed up. Are you ready for the first course?"

"Yes, I am."

"How do you want it served?"

"Hot, please."

That was the night that they heard the jaguar. His guttural growling out in the nearby jungle was a frightening experience for both of them. They waited and listened as the big cat circled the fuselage. "How did he find us?" whispered Jordanne as she clung to Alec from her position behind him.

"Followed our scent trail up from the river, I think."

"Can you shoot him?"

"No, but I'm going to try and scare him off. Cover your ears."

He pulled the gun to his shoulder and touched off a round into the trees overhead. At the blast, there was a sudden *whoof,* and the scramble of something large disappeared into the brush directly behind the fuselage. "How close was that noise?" she asked, her voice quivering.

"Five feet," he said. The cat, however, was gone.

It took them three days to plan their departure. Some of that time they spent enjoying their newfound relationship. Some of it was spent in serious discussion of what to take with them. They also idly mused about saying "to hell with it" and just stay put. Neither of them could argue seriously for that tack. They also hiked down to the river to catch fish. Alec also panned more gold.

On the morning of the third day, they bore down on the job at hand. They took it in stages. The first was hardware. They laid out what they thought they could pack. At first, it was everything. All the miscellaneous parts and pieces of the plane. A piece of broken mirror she had found. The first aid kit. The rifle and ammo. The rope. The dishes, forks, pots, and water bottles. The pickaxe, the fireman's axe, the machete. The sink for collecting rainwater. The fire starters. The gold pan. The backpack with the gold in the bottom. The shovel.

When they were finished, Jordanne stood back and surveyed all the stuff. "Holy shit!" she said. "I've heard of everything but the kitchen sink, but I'll be damned, we've got it too!"

Alec chuckled. "Not for long. That, we won't need on the river. We will have to boil water, so the pot is in. Some of the water bottles are in, but we won't need all of them. The fire starters are obvious. The rifle and ammo are in. The machete, of course. The shovel too. That leaves the parts and pieces, first aid kit, rope, dishes and utensils, pickaxe, fireman's axe and backpack, and gold pan. So what is your thinking about that stuff?"

Pleased that he had included her in the process, she went through it pulling out what she thought was essential. When she was finished, the parts and pieces, rope, and axes remained. Then he pulled out the fireman's axe and rope. At the last minute, he grabbed the pickaxe.

"Damn!" he exclaimed. "We didn't thin 'er down very much. Let's talk about why we need what we have pulled out to take. You go first."

"Well, the plates and forks are light and won't take up very much room, and they make eating possible, especially if we make stew stuff. The gold pan can hang outside the backpack. When we get out, we are going to need gold to buy our way off the coast. The first aid kit can be pared down. We don't need the box itself. The mirror, just because. I'll carry it in a pocket. So why did you pull out the axes and rope?"

"When we get down the river to where it slows down and begins ambling to the ocean, we are going to get into bamboo," he said. "We can make a raft. The rope and axe will come in handy. On our way down, I hope to pan some more gold. If it gets too burdensome to tote the axes, we can always dump them and hope to use the machete and vines to build the raft."

Still, the pile of stuff was daunting. The final list was the pot, six water bottles, fire starters, rifle and ammo, machete, shovel, first aid material, rope, mirror shard, dishes and utensils, fireman's axe, gold pan, and backpack.

The second stage was clothes. They both chose one change of pants and shirts. Both chose men's. They both stayed with the boots they had been wearing, the broad brimmed hats, and the blouses they had been tying over the hats when the bugs were thick. They each added an extra pair of socks, and she tossed in her bra.

Finally, they added their salt and pepper.

Then they began the loading of the backpack. It already weighed at least twenty pounds because of its own weight and the weight of the gold tied up in the shirt at the bottom. First came the socks and clothes, tucked in to wedge the gold in the center bottom. Next the water bottles were laid in sideways. They had decided to take four instead of six. They were followed by miscellaneous first aid items. The box of ammo was placed atop the first aid stuff, and the dishes and utensils came next. The pot and gold pan topped it off. They were both surprised that there was still a bit of room at the top. Alec worked the fireman's axe head into that space and zipped the backpack closed. He hefted it and estimated its weight at about fifty-five, maybe sixty pounds. He was pleased and relieved that it didn't weigh in the seventy-five-pound-plus class as he had feared it would.

Jordanne looked over what remained: rifle, shovel, machete, and rope. "So how do we divvy up this stuff?"

"Good question," he said. "I've got the backpack and rifle. Can you handle the machete and shovel?"

"If we can figure some way of hanging the machete from my waist, I would feel a lot better about it."

"Okay. Let's work on that. We need to figure out how to hang this rope off the back of the backpack too. I want my hands and arms free to use the rifle if I have to."

Alec took the machete over to the fuselage. He already had an idea for making a sheath for the big knife. He had noticed a length of the fuselage that was nearly torn loose. He hacked it off, measured the length needed to cover the blade, and chopped it off at that point. The piece was long enough to repeat the process. Using adhesive tape from the first aid kit, he taped the two pieces together. In opposition, the pair left a slot that the machete slid into. He then used the tape and some twine from his fishing line stock to attach a rope belt to the sheath. He cut it long enough to fit him, knowing that it would be too long for Jordanne. She would have to double knot the rope belt to keep it in place. His concern, however, was that once they had built a raft, he would need to strap on the machete himself, and that was why he had cut the rope long.

The rope problem was solved by cutting a pair of slashes in the top of the backpack and using one of their fishing lines to tie the rope into the cuts. The coils of rope were tied together at the bottom with the second line. That formed a tidy bundle, but it added five or six more pounds. The backpack weighed in at about sixty-five pounds when they were finished. Alec hefted it onto his shoulders and walked around for a bit, carrying the rifle, as well. "This is going to take some getting used to," he said. "Balancing is a bit of a struggle."

"Maybe we better not have sex until we build the raft," she offered. "You know, keep your legs under you like those football players."

He stopped and looked at her to see if she was serious. "Yeah, right," he said. "On the other hand, maybe we should stay a few days, and you can work me over to build up my strength."

"Oh, I like that idea!" she said. "Strip you naked like a gladiator. Ride you like a horse!"

"Giddy up!" he hollered.

They cooked up the last of their fish and stewed spinach for their last dinner at the fuselage. Jordanne took a half hour to visit the mass grave to say goodbye to her sister. She was strangely detached and not nearly as emotional as Alec thought she would be. In fact, their lovemaking that night was quite exuberant and arduous at times. It was also slow and tender at others. Between sessions they talked.

"Have you ever been married?" she asked.

"Oh, sure. When you are my age, you have to have tried it at least once. Mine didn't work out."

"How come?"

"Oh, after seven years, we just grew apart. We stuck it out for another year or so and then agreed to pull the pin."

"Did you have any kids?"

"Nope. She never wanted any. Stayed on the pill to make sure she didn't. That was a big part of our calling it quits."

"Did you want kids?"

"Yes."

"Did you ever think about remarrying?"

"I did, but the right girl never came along. And, as I got older, the job and other stuff just kind of got in the way. Time passed, I got over the divorce, and I just moved past that phase of my life."

"Do you still see her?"

"Not anymore. She got remarried and moved to Iowa. She has four kids now."

"How do you feel about that?"

"Well, at first, I felt betrayed. But after the second one, I just let it go. Now it doesn't bother me. I think she's happy. That's good. So how about you? Don't tell me you haven't had your chances!"

"That's a long sad story. It breaks me up to think about it, much less than talk about it, but here goes. When I finished getting my degree in physical fitness, I met Chuck. He was a hunk. Swept me off my feet. I was twenty-one, he was thirty. We shacked together for three years. I stayed on the pill, thank God. I wanted kids in the worst way, but only after we were married. There was one little problem, though. For my twenty-fourth birthday, he gave me a goodbye ring. It was goodbye Jordanne and hello Mason. I'm only just now feeling free. Feeling free of guilt. You are helping me more than you know. Now, let's make a kid."

"Whoa!" he exclaimed. "You just said you didn't want kids out of wedlock. What gives?"

"Time." She began to cry. "If I have to, I'll raise my kid on my own. I'm scarred, Alec. I don't know if I will ever be able to trust a man again. It's bad enough to lose a man to another woman. Oh, I had that happen too! But to lose the love of your life to another man is something else completely. Do you understand?"

He pulled her to him and kissed her as tenderly as he knew how. "Not right now," he said, "but my understanding is only part of what you need. You need to forgive yourself. Until you do that, you won't accept me understanding you. It will be like a piece of your puzzle that never quite falls into place. You would distrust me too. My understanding you is up to you, sweetheart. It's up to you."

She reached out for him and nestled her head into his shoulder. "I'll try if you give me the chance," she whispered. "That, and some time."

The next morning, as they were preparing to leave, Alec made an announcement that set off a row. He held up the scissors from the first aid kit. "Your hair needs to come off," he said.

"What?"

"You need to cut it short. Like a man's. We are going to run into some rough customers downriver. You need to be dressed like a man and perceived as a man. It will save us having to keep rape out of the minds of those bastards we are bound to run into. Keeping them from robbing us will be bad enough. We don't need to be stirring up their loins as well."

"Oh my god! This is giving me a headache. Maybe we should just call this whole thing off. We could get killed just trying to float down that fuckin' river!"

"Yeah, that's quite possible. But with the rifle, it's not as likely. Some of our travel will be at night. The moon phase is freshening. For several nights, we will have good light. Staying here, trying to get by on what we have found so far is just another way of dying. Slower, maybe, but just as sure."

"I don't care! The last few days have been the happiest I've had in a long, long time. I'm scared to leave, Alec. I'm scared to leave!"

With that outburst, she fell to her knees and began sobbing. He went to her and knelt before her. He wrapped his arms around her and held her for a long time. At length, she sobbed out and looked into his eyes. "Can I trust you, Alec? Can I trust you?"

As he returned her gaze, he felt his heart go. He had been holding a reserve for himself. Sensibly so. But in a twinkling, he knew she was what he wanted. He dedicated himself to her as he said, "Yes, Jordanne, you can trust me. I love you."

Her response was given in a convulsive bout of sobbing, kissing, and expressing love for each other. It finished when she said, "I will follow you to the ends of the Earth."

Finally, they shoved off. Both paused to look back at the simple camp where they had blended their hearts and souls. It didn't look much like home, but a small piece in the backs of their minds cried out at its loss. Alec found the weight of the pack distressing, and he had to stop often and work out his legs He found it funny how his legs felt like he was high stepping all around where they stopped. He exaggerated a bent-legged goose step, which delighted Jordanne, and she laughed with him. Nevertheless, he had a foreboding sense that he was leading them into dangerous experiences over which they would have little control of the consequences.

Chapter 6

They made the river at noon. Since they hadn't had any food for breakfast, they stopped and rigged up one of the fishing get-ups. Soon enough, they had a breakfast fire going. They looked at the delicious trout perfectly cooked, salted, and peppered. It made them nauseous just thinking about eating them. Jordanne was first. "When we get out of here, I'm never eating fish again," she said.

"I'm never going fishing, either." He growled. They managed to each choke down a pair of the revolting specimens. He added, "If neither of us pukes, that breakfast should get us through to tonight. Maybe we'll be far enough down to catch a different species. I'll keep a lookout for something I can shoot, but don't get your hopes up, sweetheart. It's probably going to be another fish dinner for us."

Alec kicked the fire apart and used the shovel to toss the embers and hot branches into the river. He led the way down past the familiar pools where they had fished and where Jordanne fought the big snake. At first, the way was fairly open as in an evergreen forest. They were able to skirt the rapids that separated pools of quieter water. The river, however, was picking up volume. Not only were the rapids getting larger, but they were also getting angrier with great sprays of water that spouted up over rocks that bulwarked against the onrush of the insistent river. Alec took frequent breaks. He assured Jordanne that there was no hurry. The game trail led them steadily along. Views of the river and the opposite ridge side made the day pleasant.

It was midafternoon when they were beginning to think about stopping, doing some fishing for dinner, and camping for the night. That part of the river was between pitches and was quite meadow-like. They were surprised by a herd of wild boar that came down to the river on the opposite side for water. The group was led by adult boars and sows. In all, there were approximately twenty-five animals, including the piglets. Alec and Jordanne, undiscovered or ignored by the sounder, were directly opposite on the riverbank. The pool they were preparing to fish and which was the water source for the pigs was only thirty yards wide. "Are you going to shoot one?" Jordanne queried excitedly.

"Hell, yes! I'll swim over there to retrieve it if I have to go under water to do it. Get ready. Put your hands over your ears and open your mouth."

"Are you gonna shoot a big one?"

"No. I'm going to pick off one, about half grown, that we can handle." He had sat down with his knees raised. With the rifle braced, he waited for his target to separate from the herd. When it finally turned broadside and clear, he said, "Okay, here goes." The boom of the rifle was deafening. Even the roar of the rapid just upstream was dimmed by the instant ringing in Alec's ears. The ensemble on the far bank disappeared like a vapor in a strong wind. It was, however, short by two. The target animal lay on its side kicking out its life. Just beyond it lay a piglet that Alec had not seen on the opposite side of his quarry. The piglet was an incidental kill.

"Did you get it?" Jordanne asked. She had done as instructed but had also dropped her head upon her chest and closed her eyes.

"Yeah. I got it, but I hit one of the little ones too. Damn it!"

She stood up and looked at his effort. "Is that little lump it? What are you gonna do with it?"

He looked at her to gauge her reaction. When he saw that she wasn't freaking out, he said, "Eat it."

She continued to stare across the water. "Yeah. Okay. Let's eat it. Why waste it? Right?"

"After what we have been eating, it's only fitting."

Jordanne had stepped to the edge of the pool. She turned around to see a near naked Alec shucking out of his pants. "What are you going to do?" she asked.

He had his clasp knife, the trusty tool with a four-inch blade that he had carried with him for years through thick and thin, opened and clamped in his teeth. "Swim." With that, he plunged into the pool and began stroking strongly for the opposite bank. He made it easily with only minimal downstream drift. She watched him approach the piglet first. Hiding from her the quick work he made of dressing it out, he soon had it deposited on the edge of the pool. Then he turned to his second piece of work. He turned the big pig on its back and began the gutting. Several times he had to stand up, step away, and catch his breath. Finally, he dragged it to the pool and dunked it in, sloshing it around to clean the internal cavity. When he was satisfied with that, he did the same to the piglet. He stood up, flexed his back, clamped his knife in his mouth, seized the piglet by its hind legs, and dove into the pool. He swam, holding the piglet clear of the water and stroking with just one arm. The return trip was more difficult, but not overly so. As he climbed up the bank in front of Jordanne, he heaved the piglet to the top of the bank. "I say, madam," he grinned, "would you happen to have an apple?"

She wrapped him in her arms, hugging him in delight. "No," she said softly, squeezing him, "but I do have a couple of nuts!"

"Good enough!" he returned. "Let's start a fire and see what we can roast."

While she gathered dead branches for a fire, he cut a pair of branches and trimmed them so that each had a forked end. He then searched for a branch that was three or four inches in diameter and four to five feet in length. Between them, they started a fire and planted the forked sticks into the mud on either side. He skewered the piglet with the big branch. He tied the hind legs in place. The branch extended out the pig's mouth, and there was enough leftover behind the rear legs to turn the branch over the fire. "How are you going to get the other one?" she asked.

"I'll use the rope," he said. "Keep an eye on dinner." He had untied the rope from the backpack. He slung it over his shoulder and dove back into the pool again. He made the other side easily. She watched him tie off the big pig and snug the knot. Then holding the free end of the rope, he swiftly recrossed the pool. Back on her side, he said, "Give me a hand, and we'll pull that bad boy over here."

As soon as they jerked the hog into the pool, it sank like a rock. With both of them pulling hard, they were able to keep the carcass coming and off the rock in the pool bottom. When it hit the bank, Alec rushed to the pool edge. "Keep pulling!" he shouted. He grabbed the pig by the hind legs and hauled up as hard as he could. The prize weighed roughly one hundred pounds. Still, Alec was able to drag it free of the water despite its body cavity being full of water. It was then that he discovered their bonus, so to speak. As he dragged the animal up the bank, fish began spilling out of the opening in the pig's underside.

"What the hell are those fish!" she shouted.

He began grabbing them by hand and flipping them away from the water. More than half flopped safely back into the pool, but he managed to fling a dozen onto the shore, where they flipped and flopped in the dirt. "Let's kill 'em!" he shouted, springing away as they capered about his feet. They each grabbed a branch of firewood and set about bashing the fish. Alec found that by striking a stunning blow, he could deliver the coup de gras with his knife blade. Soon, they were able to examine their catch. The fish were shaped like a pan, very deep through the belly, about eight to twelve inches long and thick across the back. They also sported a nasty set of teeth.

"So what do you think they are?" Jordanne asked again.

"Piranha," he said simply.

"My god!" she said shakily. "You swam over and back twice. Those things are vicious looking."

"So I've heard," he said, "but they are also supposed to be very tasty."

He then dragged the big pig up onto the bank. While Jordanne attended to the piglet over the fire, Alec set about processing the carcass of the bigger animal. As he worked, he piled up the discarded hide, head, and bits beside the pool. When he figured he had done all he could, he walked down to the water's edge and quickly and carefully cleaned his knife and his hands and arms. He noticed more of the fish swimming nearby as he rinsed the blood and viscera free. He donned his clothes and chuckled to himself as he glanced over at the fire where Jordanne was carefully tending to the little pig. "Hey," he called. "Come down here for a minute."

When she stepped beside him, he said, "Watch this." He then began heaving and tossing the discard pile into the pool. There was an immediate boiling frenzy of fish, some springing completely free of the water. The voraciousness of their attack was stunning in its spectacle. "That, sweetheart, is why we want to be very careful of trailing any blood in the water. Even a nick on a finger is enough. How's supper coming?"

She shuddered. "It's ready. What are going to do with those fish?"

"Let's fry up a couple and see how they taste. Might be pretty good along with the pig. The rest I'll clean, and we will dry them over the next couple of days. We are going to have to try our hand at drying this pig meat too. I think we are going to be out here for a while."

They broke out their plates and utensils. Using the dripping pig fat, Alec greased up their pot and fried a pair of the piranha. Using his knife to be sure they were done, he flaked off a good-sized bite for each of them. "Well," he said, "I never really thought I would want to try another bite of fish unless I had to, but here goes."

She watched him as he chewed for telltale signs of disgust. Seeing none, she said, "So how was it?"

"Damn! That was good." He then popped her bite into his mouth and happily chomped away while looking at her.

"Hey! That was mine." She leaned over and slugged him on the shoulder. "You greedy pig!"

He chortled and peeled off another bite, which he again popped into his mouth. "Yum!" he said happily.

At that, Jordanne pushed him out of the way and helped herself to the other fish, scooping it onto her plate with her fork. She too was pleasantly surprised at how good the fish was on her palate. By then, Alec was busy cutting pieces of meat off the suckling pig on their spit. He forked pieces onto her plate, and when he had both hers and his loaded, he paused, looked at her, and said, "Here's to the new us. Let us dine on this fine repast in commemoration of this moment. I love you! Salute!" With that, he waved a bite of the pig in the air and stuffed it into his mouth. "Oh my god!" he exulted. "This is fantastic! The only pig I'm ever gonna shoot again is a piglet."

She forked a bite into her mouth and was overwhelmed at the succulence and tenderness of the bite. "That's the only ones I'll let you shoot!" she added in delight. "This is beyond delicious." They finished their meal overeating like a pair of gluttons. There wasn't enough left of the piglet to save for breakfast, so Alec tossed the skeletal remains into the pool. Once again, the piranha boil was impressive.

"There is something else," he said as they returned from the pool and sat down by the fire.

"What's that?" she asked, staring dreamily into glowing embers beneath the licking flames.

"Well, there are pig guts over there across the river. We have our pig meat over here. We know there is a jaguar around here someplace, and there are undoubtedly meat eaters in the area, including cats, probably mountain lions. I have a feeling we are likely to have a visitor or two before morning. All this blood in the air and on the wind drifting up and down the river won't go unnoticed."

She turned to him with alarmed eyes. "Well, where do we sleep then? You are scaring the hell out of me!"

"We're in a pretty good spot right here," he said. "That downed tree behind us has a cavity facing the river. Our backs will be covered. I'll use a torch to sear out spiders or centipedes, or whatever other crawling stuff might be in there. I'll need to chop some of the roots out to clear a shooting field in front of us. Then we need to take turns staying awake. Rather than setting watches, let's stay with it until we find ourselves nodding off. Then we'll wake the other to take the next shift. The key will be to wake up the sleeper no matter whether it seems fair or not. If something comes in, shoot first, and we'll ask questions later. The sound of the shot will drive off 99 percent of anything that would come in. Don't worry about hitting it. It's probably better if you don't. I plan to fire a warning shot myself. Your shot will wake me up, and I'll take over from there. We need to do two things right now. Keeping the fire going will give a cat or other scavengers pause and give us a radius of light far enough to see to shoot, if we are threatened. So we need to pile up some firewood.

And we need to cut branches on a raised platform for a bed. I'll work on the bed if you want to gather wood."

The two worked on their jobs without wasting time or talking. Jordanne, frightened, worked with abandon. He took the machete and donned the leather gloves. After hacking off the roots he wanted removed, he took a burning branch and flamed out the cavity. Then he made a quick platform using rocks and some of the branches Jordanne had collected, plus some that he cut from small trees along the riverside.

He used the rope to weave and tie the cross members into shape. Then he tackled the job of finding branches for bedding. He finished first only because she was driven to never get enough wood. He helped for a while but called it off when he felt that they had more than enough.

"What's next?" she asked.

"We need to move our pig meat."

"Move it where?"

"To where we can keep an eye on it. It needs to be off the ground too."

"Off the ground?"

"Yeah. Try to keep ants away from it as much as we can."

"Do you know how to do that?"

"Don't have a clue. We need to brainstorm and see if we can come up with something."

"Where do these ants come from?" she asked.

"The ground as far as I know."

"Do they come down out of the trees?"

"I've heard that they clean trees, so I suppose some varieties could be tree dwellers. What are you thinking?"

"Well, why don't we hang the meat on that tree's branches?"

He looked to where she pointed. It was a tree on the edge of their camp that he had trimmed a goodly number of branches from for their bed. The branches above his trim line were heavier and unsuitable for a bed. They were stout enough to hold the meat if it were spread out far enough. "Yeah," he said. "I think you are on to something, but ants could crawl down from the top and up from the bottom."

"What stops ants?" she asked.

"Sticky stuff."

"Well, we don't have any of that stuff."

He walked over to the tree and looked it over. "You know, this tree has a lot of sap in all the cuts I made. I wonder."

He used the machete to reach up to about head high and cut a circle of branches clear of the trunk. Then he cut a line around the trunk through the bark. He repeated the cut about six inches below that. He made a vertical cut connecting the two bands and used the tip of the machete to start the process of prying the bark from the tree. Soon, he had a band of the cambium layer of the tree exposed. He tested it with his finger. "Aha!" he said, turning in triumph to Jordanne. "Sticky." He grinned.

"Won't that kill the tree?"

"Yes," he said, "but I figure it's us or the tree. And it's already doomed. Sorry about that."

"How are you going to keep them from going up from the ground?"

"Same way," he said. "Need a bigger band though. I figure the ground bunch is likely to be bigger, and there will be more of them." He proceeded to peel the bark from two feet up down to the ground, then he began hanging his pork. Where he had chunks, he used his clasp knife to fashion hinges to straddle the branches. There were some small pieces that he tossed into the pool. He used the shovel to pitch blood-soaked dirt in as well. When he had policed the area as well as he could, he stepped quickly into the pool and scrubbed his hands and arms. He also quickly stepped out as soon as he saw the fish racing toward him. He returned to the fire and sat beside Jordanne.

"Well, we are about as set as we are going to get, I think," he said. "Do you see anything else?"

"Just those fish."

"Aw, shit!" he exclaimed. "I forgot all about the fish. What do you want me to do with them?"

"At this point," she said, "just feed the fishes. I'm too tired to help, and I don't feel like getting bloody. Besides, it's almost dark, and there isn't any room left on the tree."

"Thank you. Perfect solution." He pitched the fish to the fish and watched the feeding frenzy fire up.

His awe was still in his eyes when he sat down beside Jordanne. "Damn," he said, "a man wouldn't stand a chance if he got in there with even the littlest bloody cut."

They sat close beside each other, fed the fire, and watched the sparks sail up into the deep canopy overhead. They could also see a belt of stars blazing in the brilliance of the southern hemisphere, where the view was into the middle of the Milky Way. Neither had any idea of the constellations overhead. She leaned against him. "Pretty up there." He grunted in agreement. "Do I stink?" she asked presently.

"Lift your arm, and I'll sniff your pit."

She shoved him sideways and said, "Not that way! I mean, it's been a long time since I had a chance to bathe. How do I smell?"

"Why?"

"Well, you went swimming, so you aren't likely to attract critters. I didn't. Not about to go swimming either!"

"Maybe we are just too used to each other smelling bad," he said, "because you smell just fine to me. While we are onto that, sort of, we do need to think about shortening your hair."

"I can't do that tonight. I can't even think about it."

"Well, let's see how the bed feels."

He pulled the backpack, shovel, and machete in with them. "Why do we need all this stuff in here?" she asked.

"Salt," he said. "Our sweat is an attractant to rats, porcupines, bears, and stuff I don't even know about. Miners in spike camps hang their boots from the ceiling of their tents to keep the rats from chewing through the laces."

She shuddered. "You know a bunch of shit I would just as soon you kept to yourself."

"Yeah, well," he said, "sometimes stuff is an inconvenient truth. How does the bed feel?"

"Good. Wish I had a pillow though."

He rummaged around in the backpack and drew out a pair of pants. "Roll these up," he said. "They might help."

"Yeah, they're good enough. Now, tell me how I'm supposed to sleep."

Darkness settled in. Only the constant roar of the rapids could be heard, and that eventually blended into white noise. Alec sat on a short log he had found. He was positioned in front of the bed where Jordanne lay awake. The rifle lay across his knees. He checked to see that he had loaded the magazine and slid a shell into the chamber. He double-checked to make sure the safety was on. He turned to look at Jordanne and saw her luminous eyes gazing at him.

"Hey," he said, "you need to get some sleep."

"You mean I need to be rested when I'm eaten alive?"

"No, but I want you awake to help me when I'm being eaten alive."

"Why don't we just fire off a shot every half hour?"

"Not a bad idea if we plan to stay awake all night and shoot up all our ammunition so we don't have any for tomorrow night, or the night after, or down the river, where we will probably really need it."

"Jesus! Why do men always have to think ahead? You are like every one of those I ever had anything to do with for more than a month."

"Yeah, probably so. Go to sleep."

She immediately began snoring as loudly as she could.

"Good girl," he said, "now I feel a lot better."

The night wore on, and the tension of waiting for the unknown lessened as the hours passed, and nothing happened. Alec would leave the cavity of the root ball every half hour to stoke up the fire and walk around the perimeter of their lighted area, staring into the darkness and listening for whatever might be out there moving around. He carried the rifle with him, always at the ready. He forced himself to take a longer shift than was equitable. Jordanne had finally drifted into a fitful slumber, but the bed eventually became uncomfortable, and her fear made for very little real sleep.

He did, however, decide after catching himself sound asleep with his head slumped onto his chest, for how long he didn't know, shake her gently. She was instantly wide awake. "Is there something here?" she asked, looking around with frightened eyes.

"Just a sleepy guy needing to trade places with you."

He took a moment to review with her how to handle the rifle. As she was holding it upright with the butt resting on her thigh, he was explaining some things. "First, never point this damned thing at anything you aren't going to shoot. Always, and I mean always, know where that barrel is pointed. Right now, there is a round in the chamber. This is the safety. When it's on safe, you can't pull the trigger. When you want to shoot or get ready to shoot, just flip this little lever to the left. No! Not now! And get your finger off the trigger! There is nothing here to shoot right now. Don't ever touch that trigger unless you are ready to intentionally fire the rifle! Safety is the first and last thing you think about when you handle this thing. Okay, have you got it?"

"Got it, General."

"God, I hope so. I'll probably not be able to sleep for fear of you shooting my ass off. One more thing. If you have to shoot, be sure you hold the gun solidly against your shoulder like I showed you. That thing kicks like a son of a bitch!"

Despite his concern, Alec found himself quickly falling into a deep slumber. Jordanne watched the lighted area with eyes that continually darted right and left. She would imagine she heard something, pull the rifle up and point it in the direction of the imagined noise, and hold her breath interminably. When nothing came out of the darkness, she would sag down and drop the rifle to arms' rest. When she tended the fire, she overdid it, building the campfire into a small bonfire. After an hour, she realized that at the rate she was throwing wood on the fire, the stockpile would be gone well before daylight. She didn't patrol the perimeter either. As soon as she had fed the fire, she retreated quickly to the relative safety of her bunker. She kept a close eye on Alec, secretly hoping he would wake up refreshed and spend the rest of the night with her all the while taking over charge of the gun. She knew there would be no sleeping for her for the remainder of that night.

The big cat came out of the darkness from upriver. He walked on the far side of the fire toward the river. The fire seemed not to bother him very much, although he skirted it, keeping in the edge of darkness without actually wading in the water. He seemed to know exactly where the pig meat was located, and his gait was assured and steady as he walked a circular path around the fire, keeping carefully in the gloom just beyond the campfire light. Jordanne was amazed. One moment he wasn't there, and the next he was. He swung his great head toward her as she gasped. He stopped, and his eyes gleamed like meteors stilled in flight. That he was magnificent didn't enter her mind. She saw only the harbinger of death. Her scream and the crack of the rifle were simultaneous. Alec was instantly by her side. "What is it?" he asked frantically. He quickly scanned the entire half circle of light cast from the fire. There was nothing there.

Jordanne, trembling into near convulsions, pointed to where the great beast had stood looking at her. "Right there! It was right there."

"What was it?"

"I don't know. It was big and striped, and it looked right at me. I've never been so scared in my life. Not even when that snake had me."

"Did you hit it?"

"I don't know. Maybe. It seemed like the barrel was pointed at it, but as soon as I pulled the trigger, it was gone."

Alec carefully took the gun, set it aside, and wrapped her in his arms. As she slowly calmed down and stopped shaking, he said, "You did good, sweetheart. You did real good." After, he reloaded the rifle, and with it in his right hand and a flaming branch in his left, he examined the area she had indicated. He found a small splotch of blood on the ground and the marks where the great cat had turned and leaped the pool to the opposite side of the river. "You hit it," he called over his shoulder.

"I did?" she asked from a step directly behind him.

Startled, he said, "Jesus, don't sneak up on me like that!"

"I didn't. I'm not going to sit over there all alone. I've been right behind you all along."

"Okay, okay, all right," he said. "It's just that you have an alarming way of showing up when I don't expect it. Scares me shitless! Just let me know where you are at times like this."

"Boo!" she shouted.

He jerked back a step. "Damnit, Jordanne! Are you bound and determined to give me a heart attack?"

She laughed. "You're too easy. Wait till I fire that rifle when there's no reason to!"

He looked at her. "You can't be serious."

"Probably not, but I get urges."

"Well, save your urges for someone else next time. I'm about urged out. Let's take a look at your blood spot."

"What does it mean?" she asked.

They stood looking as Alec swept a burning branch around the site of the blood. "I'm not sure, but I don't think it was more than a graze. In the morning, I'll go across the river and see if there's a blood trail. Maybe I can get a better read over there."

"I don't want to be left alone, Alec," she said.

"Don't worry, you'll have the rifle. Just don't shoot at me when I come back in."

First light found them both asleep. He was facing out, and she was cuddled in against and behind him. The fire was burned down to embers. A shorebird that had flown down to perch on a tree branch hovering over the river let out with a raucous shriek. It caused Alec to open his eyes. "Damnit!" he muttered vehemently to himself. "I only wanted to help Jordanne get a little sleep." He swung his feet around and anxiously looked at their meat tree. About a third of it was gone. "Son of a bitch!" he exclaimed.

"What's the matter?" she asked sleepily.

"I fell asleep, and something got a bunch of our meat."

She was instantly panicked. "Did that cat I shot come back?"

"I don't know. I'll have to look for tracks. I just woke up and saw that we were robbed. Damn me to hell. I fell asleep!"

His examination showed that a different cat, maybe more than one had come in and pulled meat off the lower branches. He didn't think it was the jaguar. He couldn't find pug marks, and the ground was soft enough to show them as heavy as the big cat obviously was. He concluded that smaller cats had been the invaders.

Jordanne had also arisen, but she checked herself from walking up behind Alec, although she was nervous about being away from his side. She waited as he returned. "It wasn't your cat," he said.

He stoked up the fire and retrieved some pork from the tree. "I'll fry up some of this for breakfast," he said, "but after gutting the owner, I doubt it will be anything like the piglet."

It wasn't. Both tried their best, but they finally admitted they were simply trying to brave it through. "So what are we gonna do with the rest of that crap?" she asked.

"Two choices. Leave it in the tree. Toss it in the river."

"Well, I'll bet those fish haven't had a thing to eat since last night. Poor things are probably starving."

"You know this puts us back on the fish diet," he said.

"Those piranhas aren't bad."

"Well, there won't be any of those," he said. "All they would do with our fishing gear is snap off the hooks. We'd never catch one."

Alec took the rest of the pig, tossed it into the piranha pool, and watched the fish boil again. Then he examined the blood spot. In the daylight, he found a tuft of hair and decided that the cat had indeed only been grazed. "Will it live?" Jordanne asked over his shoulder.

Startled, Alec turned quickly. "Didn't see you there. Yes, it will live. You only grazed it, so I don't think there's any point in me swimming over there to check for a blood trail. I think we should load up and get on down the river pretty soon. I want to check out a couple of those gravel bars upstream to see if we can find any more gold. We aren't going to have a lot of chances once we get off this river. I don't think the cat will be back tonight, but I'd rather not be around to find out."

"Roger that," she said. "I will not miss the encore."

Alec took the pickaxe and shoved a branch for a handle into the eye, used the machete to hack some wedges from another branch, tapped them in with a rock, and tested it. He was satisfied with the result. He emptied out the backpack, except for the gold he had already panned. Then he grabbed his gold pan and headed upstream. Jordanne stretched out with her face to the sun and took a nap.

For two hours, he worked at a fever pace. By the time he felt compelled to quit, he figured he had a total accumulation of about thirty pounds of gold. *My god,* he thought happily, *if I can get this stash out of here, it's half a million. But, brother, that's a huge* if.

He hoofed it back to their camp and shared his haul with Jordanne. "Half a mil," he said, grinning like a gold miner. She was happy to see him happy as he tore apart their bed to save their rope.

"How hard will it be getting our gold out of here?" she asked.

He glanced at her to see how serious she was. "Life and death if it's discovered. This kind of treasure will draw killers. We will be killers too. In self-defense, but killers, nevertheless."

"You expect me to kill someone when I've only fired a gun once in my life? Are you crazy?"

"Maybe, but wait for it. When you are looking at a bastard like those we are likely to see on the river who wants to rape you and kill me, you will change your mind."

"Is this all really worth it?"

"At some point, no. It's worth a chance, though, sweetheart, it's worth a shot. If it all goes to hell, we'll reconsider."

The two of them loaded the pack, tied on the rope, and divided up the carry items as they had the day before. "How far are we going today?" she asked.

"Don't know how far. Getting started now, though, we should get in eight hours."

"Love you, dear, but there's no way you are going to pack that thing for eight hours. Besides, today I want a bath."

"I'll be your towel boy."

"We don't have those."

"Even better."

Their hike was similar to the day before. They followed game trails as much as they could, detoured when tributaries came pouring down the ridge. They made their way slowly down the river valley.

Again, they made frequent rest stops. They took time to build a fire at midmorning because they had drained the last of their water. Using their pot, they boiled water and let it cool. They both drank their fill and then filled their water bottles. Resuming their trek, they continued for another three hours or so. They had found a small glade below a rapid, and alongside, a long pool being held back by a rock spine that spanned the river, almost like a dam. They could hear the moan and bellow of the next rapid below them. Alec looked around and sized the place up. "I don't know about you, but I'm bushed. This is the first place like this we've seen all day. We aren't likely to find a place any better. What say we camp here for the night?"

"Hallelujah!" She dropped down to the ground and sat on her butt. "I was beginning to think you'd never stop. We've been at this since daylight, and we haven't eaten anything all day but that wretched pig meat. The vote's unanimous. Let's make camp."

While she scouted around for firewood, he began the work of building a crude shelter and bed. Again, he used rocks and branches thick enough to hold their bed off the ground. The bed was built up against the side of a downed log. He used the rope as he had the night before. Boughs were again laid atop the bed. When he had that completed, he cut pieces to lay across the log in a lean-to fashion to form a shelter. Then he cut more branches and boughs to form a roof. This took him several hours. For the last two hours, she helped lugging branches and tossing them onto the lean-to. "Why are we putting so many branches on this thing?" she asked.

He stopped and pointed up. Above them, the clouds were darkening and thickening. "Oh," she said. "The shower room will be opening soon."

"Yes, and it's going to be open for quite a while. You do still have your soap, don't you?"

"How did you know?"

"I saw you roll it into your extra socks."

"You aren't going to take it out on me, are you?"

"Oh, yes, I am. You've got to share."

"Only if you promise to do my back," she said in mock severity.

"I can handle that!" he said. "Yes indeed, I can handle that."

They finally piled all the branches onto their lean-to that they felt made sense. It stood like a small green haystack at the edge of the glade. "I doubt it will keep the rain out, but we can hope," he said. The two of them undressed and laid their clothes on the bed. Soon after, the rain commenced. At first, it was a soft embrace, but it built into a downpour that eased into a steady rain that lasted for hours. The two of them shared the soap and the joy of soaping each other up. Without towels, they crawled into their lean-to and drip dried as much as they could. They dressed and pulled extra clothes out of the bag. The temperature had dropped with the storm, and both of them were getting cold. After an hour, the shelter leaked everywhere, and they got wet. "I've got to try to start a fire," he told her. "I'll need your help."

Alec had dragged a goodly portion of their firewood into the shelter, hoping to keep some of it dry. He used his clasp knife and the machete to build up a pile of shavings from branches that were wet but dry inside. He had emptied the backpack so Jordanne could hold it over him to keep the wood from getting wetter than it already was. When he had enough shavings, he used a fire starter to light his fire. He blew on the shavings as he added small pieces of branches and bits he had split off bigger branches. It worked. He managed a big enough fire to overcome the dripping through the branches. He had built the fire to the lee end of the shelter, so the smoke blew in the direction of the storm on the slight breeze that accompanied it. When he had arm-sized branches burning, he continued to feed small pieces in at the base of the blaze. Using the machete, he chopped the wood into pieces that he was sure would survive the overhead dripping. It wasn't comfortable, but he figured they could survive if the storm didn't last all night.

They spent a wet night, neither getting much sleep. Alec had a short piece of broken tree branch big enough to sit on. He pointed it at the fire, straddled it, and had her sit in front of him so she could lean back into him, and he could hold her in his arms. She was able to drowse and get some rest. He had to rouse her to feed the fire from time to time. Sunrise came with both of them exhausted. She woke and found his head had slumped on her shoulder. For how long, they didn't know, but he didn't feel at all rested.

The day was splendid—washed and fresh with a shining sun sparkling off the water, where it broke over the rocky spine angling across and down to the head of the next big rapid. The river directly before them was a long pool with a discernible current. "You hungry?" he asked.

"I could shoot and cook you," she said.

"I guess I better try that pool then."

"I thought you said piranha would bite off the hooks."

"There is a good current right here. Maybe the piranha don't like that. Worth a try." He used the shovel to dig for worms. It took a while, but he finally turned over four. He stuffed three in a pocket of his pants. He cut a suitable tree branch using the machete. He trimmed it into a fairly stout six-foot length, tied off one of their fishing lines, baited the hook, and slowly approached the edge of the pool in a crouched stance. He dunked the worm into the water, but the current swept it away on the surface. "Gotta have some weight." He grunted to himself, standing up and swinging the pole up and away from the water. It banged into Jordanne, who was standing behind and slightly to his right. Once again, he was surprised and startled to see her where she wasn't expected. "Jordanne, I'm going to start calling you Ghost if you keep sneaking up on me. What are you doing?"

"Ha, very funny," she said. "I'm watching and learning in case you take a bullet, and I have to get out of here on my own."

"That's a comforting thought," he said. "I hope you're not planning on shooting me and taking the gold all to yourself."

"Hadn't thought of that, but it brings up a point. If we run into those river runners you talked about, our gold will be a liability. Now what are you looking for?"

"I need a rock I can tie into the line. I get your point about the gold, but on the other hand, it might be an asset. We'll just have to wait and see." He searched the shoreline of the pool and presently found a piece of limestone that was about three inches long and shaped like a finger. It proved to be what he wanted. With it tied securely about two feet above the hook, he was able to hold the worm steady in the stream of the pool about three feet deep. Both crouched low beside the pool, she just behind him. Within seconds, his pole was suddenly jerked and nearly pulled from his hand. He quickly stood up and shouted, "I'm going to swing it onto the bank. Grab it so it doesn't flop back in!"

Carefully, he pulled his catch toward shore, pulling it up toward the surface. When he had it two feet from the edge, he gave it an extra heave. A wildly struggling fish, not a piranha, flopped mightily on the bank. Jordanne pounced on it. "Got it!" she shouted.

He quickly moved to assist her in subduing the fish and seeing what it was. He had carried a piece of firewood to use as a fish stunner, and he bashed the head of the fish three or four times until he was sure it had expired. What it was, he had no idea. It didn't have a face full of teeth, and he was able to carry it by gripping its lower lip. It was the biggest fish they had caught and more than enough for a meal for both of them. He pulled out his magic book and began searching for the fish's identity. Jordanne, on the other hand, planted the fish on their log seat and said, "Toss me your knife." He looked up, saw what she wanted, and pulled out his clasp knife.

"Here you go," he said. Shortly, he closed the book. "It's a peacock bass," he announced. "My very first. And according to my book, very good eating."

"Wonderful, Mr. Isaac Walton. But I could use some help here. This sucker is a lot harder to gut than trout and piranha."

"I got it," he said, moving in to take over. The fish weighed seven or eight pounds and was distinctly striped with broad vertical dark stripes on a gold background. He completed the gutting process and carried the fish to the pool where he washed it and removed the bloodline inside the cavity and up against the backbone. When he returned to their shelter, he found she had a good bed of embers spread out.

"Jesus, that's a big fish!" she exclaimed. "How do we cook it? It's way too big for our plates or pot."

The machete was propped against the side of the bed. He reached over and drew it slowly and dramatically to him. "Observeth, my beauty," he said, "and learneth from thy mathter!"

Positioning the bass on the small log, he slammed the machete down, just forward of the broad tail fin, clipping it neatly free of the carcass. Then he pushed down on the back of the fish, spreading it astraddle against the wood. With another blow, he lopped off a four-inch chunk. He repeated until he chunked six portions of approximately the same length. Those toward the center and head of the fish were much heavier. He figured to cut some spitting sticks from some willows he had seen upstream from their glade. "I'll be right back, sweetheart." He smiled happily. "Breakfast right away."

The fish proved to be excellent table fare. Both agreed that if push came to shove, they could do just fine eating peacock bass. They also agreed to stay in their camp until they had eaten most of the bass. Alec figured a couple of days. He was trying to figure a way to cook the bass, so they had at least a day of traveling food. He shared his thoughts with her. "Is there any room at all in the backpack?" she asked.

"Yeah, we could cram some pieces into the top, but it would make a mess that would undoubtedly drop bits of fish down into our clothes."

She opened the pack and dug deep toward the bottom. Presently, she presented him her bra. "Here you go. Put a piece of fish in each one of the cups and thank your lucky stars your girlfriend has a thirty-four-inch bust with a D cup!" she said proudly.

"Really?" he said. "So that's what I've been fooling around with. Wow, who knew?"

"You are hopeless," she said. "Here, you have lived for half a century, and you take something for granted that most men would crawl a mile on their hands and knees just to look at."

"Can I claim ignorance as bliss?"

She walked in front of him, threw her shoulders back, and said, "Yes, you can, honey. Now kiss me and get busy cookin'."

For the next couple of hours, they toasted and roasted their fish. She kept reassessing in her mind the circumstances that threw them together. She wondered if, when the stress of their current situation was over, they would still have any interest in staying together. Her hope was a wavering blend of reality, desire, and uncertainty. She knew it would all settle down suddenly when they were back in civilization, if they got that far. The best she could do before circumstance and fear interfered with the moment was to compartmentalize her doubt as best she could. That she loved him more deeply than any man she had known before would do for now.

For his part, he was determined to process the fish into a smoked and dried state that would hold for at least a few days. He experimented, filleting some of the chunks, removing the bones as best he could, and trying to overcook the product without burning it. "Damn it!" he exploded when he lost a nice piece down into the middle of the fire. "Do you have an idea on how to do this?"

"Well," she said, grinning at him impishly, "you could always catch more fish. In two or three days, you'd have enough to fill up the bra."

"Ho ho ho! A lot of help you are. Why don't you try it for a while?"

"I watched a film in grade school one time of the Indians drying fish. They used a rack. Does that help?"

He looked at her and thought a bit. Nodding, he said, "Hell, yeah. I saw films like that too. I think I can rig up a rack so we can give it a try." He took the machete and set about fashioning a rack. He used vines he pulled from a tree to tie in the cross members. He leaned it over a small smoky fire, loaded the rack with fish, and sat back to watch the result.

He didn't pay attention to Jordanne. He barely noticed her wander out of sight. When he saw she was gone, he carefully and quickly pulled his rack off the fire and set it aside. Then he grabbed the rifle and machete. He wasn't really sure which direction she had headed. His best guess was downstream. He remembered seeing her mosey in a distracted way behind him and slightly in the downstream direction. He also guessed that having come from upstream, she would be less curious about what lay in that direction. He took to the faint game trail and ran as much as he could, working his way over fallen down trees of all sizes, fighting through brush and vines. The further he went, the more concerned he became. He began calling her name as loudly as he could. He stood in place, calling in all directions. After fifteen minutes, he figured she had to be back behind him. He began to think of possibilities. The range of those was like a rainbow. At length, he decided stealth was better than bluster. It took him a good deal longer to return, and when he was within sight of the camp, he was horrified to see Jordanne, the apparent captive of a pair of men. Both were scruffy, apparent river rats. She was trying to fend one of them off. He was trying to kiss her as she bent backward, twisting her face to the side. His hand was pressing her breast upward as he struggled to push her off her feet. The other was rifling through the backpack. "Hey, what have we here!" he exclaimed. He had found the gold in the bottom of the pack and was examining a pair of the largest nuggets. "This is gold!"

The mugger whirled, his obsession with Jordanne temporarily interrupted. "Let me see that!" he demanded. Alec dropped the machete and stepped into the open with the rifle raised to his shoulder. Jordanne saw him. With his left hand, he waved her away. She darted aside, then sprinted for the trees. "Hey, get back here, bitch!" the mugger shouted, pulling a revolver from a side holster and firing a wild shot at her.

Alec was steadily moving, unnoticed by the pair. He stopped twenty feet away, the rifle holding steady between the pair. "Hold it!" he bellowed. The pair spun toward him. The one who had fired the potshot at Jordanne, without giving it a thought, fired quickly at Alec. The shot missed. His didn't. The man was blown completely off his feet and into his partner. That fellow threw down the backpack, stumbled from under his partner, and sprinted from beneath the lean-to and down the river. In an instant, he was gone. In his left hand, he clutched two gold nuggets.

Alec moved cautiously toward the man he had shot. First, he kicked the man's foot. There was no response. Then he prodded him with the rifle barrel. It was clear the bastard was dead. Alec stared, stunned. Dread thoughts cascaded through his brain. He was unable to move, except for dropping the rifle. Then Jordanne was in his arms. She was crying in relief, horror, and disbelief for both of them. They stood, clutching each other; for how long, neither knew. At last, time quit standing still. They found themselves seated on the short log.

"God, oh my god!" Alec began. "Where do we begin? How did you run into those two?"

"I was looking for gold," she said. "They were on me before I saw them. There is a big tree across the river in the middle of the next rapid. I think they crossed from the other side to this side on that tree. Next to the river, you can't hear a thing. They came out of the brush and grabbed me. I struggled until one of them pressed a gun under my chin. They started hustling me back here. They must have known this clearing is here. They kept telling me what they were going to do to me as soon as they got me here where they could lay me down. The lean-to made them slow down. Then you showed up."

Alec looked at her and said quietly. "You're all right now. You can't imagine how I felt watching that son of a bitch paw you. I would have shot him even if he hadn't shot at me. I'm going to bury him up in the trees so deep nobody will ever find him. And I'll never look back."

"I'll help you dig," she said.

Chapter 7

The following day, the two completely removed all vestiges of their camp. When they were finished, there was no sign they had ever been there. Even the campfire was gone, thrown shovelful by shovelful into the river, buried the same way, and covered over with duff. When he repacked the pack, Alec carefully bundled their gold into one of the arms of a shirt he had cut off and tied at both ends, using one of their fishing lines. The very top of the pack was crowned with her bra, packed with dried fish. Alec had devoted himself to his drying rack the previous afternoon and night. The fish had dried beautifully.

"Why do you suppose those two were crossing the river on that tree?" Alec asked Jordanne as they were getting set to leave. "Let's go check that out." It took a while for them to struggle alongside the river down to the big tree. It had fallen off a rise that concealed the way ahead. As they breasted the rise, they were shocked to see that their river had plunged off its last rapid and into another river. The new one was ten, perhaps twenty, times the size of their own.

"Are we getting somewhere?" Jordanne asked.

"Well, we are on one hell of a big river. Unless I miss my guess, this one flows all the way to the sea. And look at this trail we're standing on. It's a path used by people. That's what those two were doing, walking on this path. Why? I have no idea. I do wonder where the one that got away went, however. Say, did you notice something about those two?"

"Yeah. I noticed several somethings! What did you think?"

"Not that. I don't think either were Latino."

"What does that mean?"

"Drugs."

"Are you serious?"

"I think so. We must be in Colombia. Drugs here are like potatoes to Idaho. It's the country's cash crop. Maybe their only crop. So, my loved one, your hair has to go."

"Christ! What if I tell you to go to hell?"

"That was mild enough. Maybe I have a chance to get you to see reason."

"Don't go over all that again. I don't need to hear it! Give me a piece of that fishing line we had left after you tied off the gold pouch."

He dropped the backpack and pulled out the line. "Here," he said.

She took it, removed her hat, and pulled her hair straight up on her head. Somehow, in a way he couldn't comprehend, she tied a ponytail that was atop her head. She donned her hat and brushed the hair that fell across her face back to the side. She looked like a boy with blonde hair, a little too long, stringing out under his hat. "What do you think?" she queried as she pirouetted around a couple of times.

"Well, I have to agree. That problem is solved. But my buxom, bouncing boy, there is another problem I hadn't thought about."

"My tits! Damn! I hadn't thought about that, either. I'll have to bind 'em."

"How do you do that?"

"Just like you did when you bound my ribs. You get to help again, you lucky dog, you!"

"Just show me how, my love. I am your blushing handmaiden!"

They used the shirt missing a sleeve, cut strips from the rest of it, and wrapped her, snugly tying the strips down the middle of her back. That was Alec's job. Several times, she sharply told him to pull tighter. "Jesus, Jordanne, I trying to flatten your tits, not break your ribs," he groused.

"Just shut up and pull!" she retorted. "I'll let you know if you're pulling too hard. Right now, you aren't flattening anything. Just pull, damnit!"

At last, the job was done. She put her man's shirt back on and turned around a time or two. "So?" she asked.

"Boy," he said. "You look like an eighteen-year-old boy. How do you feel? Can you breathe?"

"Not as well, but good enough. We do need to build that raft you talked about, however. Soon."

They hiked the new trail down the river all that day. It was much easier going, and where tributaries poured in off the side hill, there were crossings. Some required wading, and some were a tree or multiple trees that served as foot bridges. Alec pushed himself hard. He wanted to get away from the shooting scene as soon as possible. The only stops were for lunch and a few when his legs just gave out under the burden of the deadweight backpack. He kept a nervous watch for traffic on the river and for other foot travelers. It was dusk when he finally started looking for a suitable spot to camp for the night. He chose a hillock that sloped moderately down and across the trail. He turned uphill and climbed until he crested and went down the backside. There, in a small clearing, he removed the backpack and announced, "No fire tonight."

Jordanne responded, "I'm too tired to care, Bwana. How many more days like this do you have in mind?"

"Good news, on that front," he announced. "We are into bamboo now. Tomorrow, we work on our raft."

"Thank Christ!" she exclaimed.

"I was wondering, for the record," he asked, "when you said you were looking for gold when you were ambushed, did you find any?"

"Maybe I did, and maybe I didn't. What's it to you?"

"Business."

"Business! Would you stop with innuendo and say what I can understand?"

"Well, I was going to save this for later. But I guess this is as good a time as any. That guy that got away from us left with some of our gold. There is a pretty good chance that when he reveals it, there will be a stampede for our river. I think that's our gold up there where we picked and panned it, so I was wondering just how far downstream the gold is spread. I'm also thinking about returning and getting more. What do you think?"

"I think you're fucking nuts!"

He chuckled. "That's for granted, but Jesus, sweetheart, wasn't that wonderful getting all that gold? We must have twenty-five pounds or more in our pouch. At twelve troy ounces to the pound and eighteen hundred per ounce, we have approximately a half million dollars if we can get it out of here. What I'm thinking is that if we can get back in there, even if there is a rush, we should be able to triple that in a month. If we supply up, we will have it a lot better than when we were there. Won't be easy, but think of it! In a couple of months, we could be lounging at the Holiday Inn in Miami, sipping Mai Tai's with millions in the bank."

Jordanne stood up from where she had plopped down, reached into her pocket, and pulled out four pickers about the size of marbles. "Here," she said. "This is my contribution to your scheme. I ain't going back there, and you are still fucking nuts."

"Here," he said, "have a piece of fish. I'm going to bed."

They cuddled for warmth and simply spread out on the ground on a bed of boughs he cut for a bed. As tired as they were, both slept fairly well. When they returned to the trail in the morning, he kept a lookout for a place where they could get far enough away from the trail to work without attracting attention and where there was a good stand of heavily shafted bamboo near a beach of the river. Finding it wasn't easy, and it was midafternoon before he found it. A boisterous tributary forced the trail upslope nearly a half mile. He led the way across and then turned down off the trail and heading to the river. He used the machete to clear the way after he felt they were far enough off the footpath for his hacking not to be seen by passersby. They bushwhacked for nearly an hour before he broke through, forcing his way through a lush bamboo thicket and onto a beach some thirty feet wide. As Jordanne squeezed through the last of the bamboo, she found him looking around and grinning happily. "Look at this," he enthused. "It's perfect!"

"Wonderful," she said. "Where's my Mai Tai?"

He turned to her and laughed. "Hold that thought. Come here." He held her, gazing into her eyes. "I promise you," he said, "I will not put you in jeopardy, intentionally, no matter what happens to us."

"Somehow I feel like you are keeping a shoe in the air," she said, kissing him regardless. "Now you can do something for me."

"What's that?" he asked.

"Help me unbind. I feel like I have been kicking my tits with my knees for a week."

They took time to set up a semi-permanent camp. Alec assembled the fire axe. He used a four-foot stem of bamboo, ran it through the eye of the axe, and plugged it with a piece of branch that he drove in place using a rock for a hammer, tightening the handle securely. The bamboo lent itself to easier construction of a bed platform and a rude shelter. While he began cutting, he sent her in search of vines that could be used to bind the framework of both structures together. He figured to finish first but was surprised when she came back with a surprising bundle of vines coiled like a rope and slung over her shoulder. "That was quick," he said. "What have you got there?" He reached down to where she had shrugged the coil to the ground and pulled a loose end up. He pulled to test its strength and found it parted rather easily. She had turned to look at the river, arching her back with her hands on her hips, and then leaning down till her nose touched her knees.

"That feels better," she said, turning around. He was testing another section of vine. "No!" she shouted. "Not that way. Give me that! Why can't you wait for a minute before you go bull rushing into things?"

"Well, excuse me!"

"You're going to ruin it that way. This is how you do it." She pulled a length off the coil, doubled it, and twisted it. "Here, pull that apart."

He took it and carefully pulled it in contrary directions, trying not to tear it in two too easily. He didn't want to upset her any more than he already had. He kept steadily adding more and more pressure until he maxed himself out. "Wow!" he said. "How did you figure that out?"

"Magic," she said, "but for some sex, I will reveal all."

"Let me get back to building that bed!"

For the next several days, the two of them enjoyed themselves: constructing their raft, sleeping in the afternoons, and fishing with new bamboo rods that reached fifteen feet into the water. Alec also found edible bamboo shoots that they could soften in water and then stew with bits of fish. The raft was a matter of discussion: its size by width and length, should it have a steering oar, what about paddles? A railing, a hut. When it was all said and done, they did it all. The raft was ten by twelve feet. The bamboo planks were six to eight inches in diameter, lending excellent stability. Alex was obsessed with strapping it together with the vines that Jordanne continued to gather. He feared having it come apart on the water. When it was finished, they used bamboo poles cut to twelve feet to pole it next to the riverbank upstream for a couple hundred yards. The sweep oar was ten feet long. Alec had weighted it with rock to keep it from twisting as he experimented with how it moved the raft. It was a huge success. Both tried the big oar and felt quite smug about how they could steer the raft. A final touch was to attach a raised twelve-inch section of bamboo to the bow and along each side at the bow and stern to serve as cleats. Alec had found a flat rock, for which Jordanne wove a vine basket. He attached a length of rope to it, and they had an anchor.

A day later, they loaded up and shoved off. He had tied off a length of rope to the bow cleat so that they could beach the raft at night. Floating the river was idyllic for two days. Both were thankful not to have to struggle up and down the ridge hemming the river. Jordanne was especially relieved not to be bound. What they regretted the most was having run out of salt. Then they started spotting people on the bank side trail. At first, the people followed along out of apparent curiosity. They gathered on the riverbank where the trail dipped to its edge. There they stood and watched silently as the raft floated past. Jordanne waved at them in a friendly way. The children would shyly look at their parents and meekly raise their hands, then duck out of sight. It was quite charming. Even Alec would smile largely and touch his hat brim like he was in a western movie.

Then there was the group that was armed. Fortunately, they were well above the river's edge and moved into screening cover without noticing the raft. It gave Alec time to move well offshore. Jordanne was frightened and asked, "Were those drug runners?"

"Maybe. They could have been local militia too. I doubt they look too much different. I hate to say this, but we need to put you back into disguise."

"Crap, I knew this was too good to last. All right, let's get it over with."

The next morning, after spending a restless night where they had pulled into a back eddy and anchored offshore, they coasted carefully into a squalid-looking native village. Jordanne asked, "What do you think the name of this place is, Huck?"

"Gee, Tom, I don't know. Let me guess. Quarter horse shithole."

"Do you have something against horses?"

"Sorry. Half horse shithole."

"That's better. What are we doing here.?"

Alec looked around. "Looking for salt and some other stuff. Do you speak Spanish?"

"Not a lick."

"All righty, then," he said, "let's toss the anchor onto shore to hold us in place and see what gives."

When they had anchored, he stepped ashore and looked at the assemblage before him. The people were small in stature. The children were naked. The adults wore loin cloth, like diapers and dresses that looked like sarongs. All a dirty white. Alec smiled broadly, bowed, and looked for someone of authority. Seeing no one like that, he pointed to himself. "*No hablo Espanol,*" he said. "*Tu hablo Engles?*" His question was to no one in particular, and he wasn't sure he had asked properly if anyone there spoke English. He waited. The natives waited. Then Alec asked, "Sal?"

At that, one of the men shook his head. "No sal."

Alec nodded and said, "Mucho gracias. Hasta la vista." He turned to the raft, heaved the anchor on board, smiled happily, and used one of their pry poles to shove the raft out into the current of the river.

"That went well," Jordanne offered. "I have to say, you sounded impressive. What did you say?"

"Well, I think I said I don't speak Spanish, and I asked if anyone spoke English, and I asked for salt, and he said no salt, and I said thank you very much and goodbye."

"Ah," she said.

Later, as they floated quietly offshore a hundred yards, Jordanne spotted something swimming in the water. It was heading through a weed bed toward shore. "What's that?" she asked.

"I think it's a capybara," he said. "I'm going to take a shot at it."

"No, you don't!"

"It's red meat, and we could use it. I'm starved for something besides fish."

"So am I, but I don't want to draw attention to us with that bunch with rifles up there somewhere who could make red meat out of us!"

"Damn! You're right. Woo, look at that," he said. "It ain't capybara now." As he spoke, a wild thrashing of water occurred, and the animal was pulled underwater by something they couldn't see. It did not resurface.

"What was that?" she asked.

"Not sure. Not a snake. Maybe a caiman or a croc."

Jordanne had been sitting on the edge of the raft, trailing her lower legs in the water. She quickly pulled her legs out of the water. "Did you know there are crocs in this river?"

"Only generally. I saw some pictures in my book, so yeah, I suppose if I'd thought about it, I would have known if you had asked."

"You are impossible sometimes! Do you know that? If I didn't love the hell out of you, I'd push you off this raft and let you swim for it."

"The book's in the backpack. Help yourself. Become knowledgeable."

"I can't believe this. I never liked biology, now I have to study it to figure out what's gonna eat me."

"Oh, there isn't anything going to eat you."

"That reminds me," she said, "you owe me a snake. Or did you forget about the one that tried to eat me.?"

"Sure, bring up ancient history. Are you gonna be like this always?"

"Only as long as you hang around, honey. Only as long."

For the rest of the day, they floated along. She studied his book. He kept them well into the strength of the current. He was really enjoying his raft. It was solid, stable, and responsive. They hadn't encountered rapids, so he wasn't sure how it would fare there, but as a craft on big quiet water, it was a beauty. He studied the shoreline for a spot to pull in for the night. They needed to do some fishing and boil some water. "Hey, my little bookworm," he said, "do you feel like doing a little fishing on the way to camp?"

"Okay," she answered. "I have only identified about a hundred things that could kill me and fifty that can eat me. Maybe I can hook one this afternoon."

"Well, drag it on the raft so after it eats you, I can eat it."

"Will do, Captain Ahab. Where's my bait?"

"Let me look in the trusty cup. Well, yes, we have two worms in the left cup. Let me set you up."

She trailed the line off the left side of the raft near the stern. The additional length of the twelve-foot bamboo rod kept the bait well away from the shadow of the raft and away from the slow sweep of the steering oar as Alec kept the raft positioned squarely in the current. At first, Jordanne watched her line intently for any sign of a bite or a nibble. She held her rod at a thirty-degree angle and occasionally dipped it down toward the water and then back up as she made the worm seem to be more than just a dead thing hanging in the water. But she eventually grew bored and laid the rod on the deck and draped a leg over it. She leaned back on her hands and craned her head back, enjoying the sun on her face. She was daydreaming about simple things like the conveniences of home in America. What she had taken for granted was amazing to her. Daily showers, electric appliances, any kind of food she wanted any time she wanted it. She thought of her clothes closet in her apartment in Phoenix. She counted the money in her savings, checking, and IRA. She wondered about the value of her small stock portfolio. It startled her that those things which had been so important and fundamental to her, she had not thought of since the crash of the plane. She looked at Alex and wondered if she really meant it when she said, "I will follow you to the ends of the Earth."

Then the fish struck. The bamboo pole dipped violently and popped up beneath her leg. It was just leaving the raft when she caught it in a lunge with her left hand. "I've got something!" she shouted.

Alec looked toward her and saw she was nearly off the raft. Quickly, he laid the big oar down and jerked it snug against the stern. "Hang on!" he yelled. He dove and caught her around the waist just as she was about to go over. He tugged her back. Whatever it was on her line tugged her back. "Don't let go of the pole," he yelled again, and, reaching around her, grabbed the dancing bamboo with her. Suddenly the fish jumped, clearing the water and shaking its head in an effort to throw the hook. In appearance, the fish was long, dark green, but shaded to red toward its tail.

"What is it?" Jordanne cried.

"Arapaima!" he hollered gleefully. "A little one, but he'll do! Don't lose him. I'm going to get the fish bat." He scooted over to their sleeping hut and pulled from the underside of their bed a three-foot piece of bamboo that was three inches in diameter. He had plugged the end of it with a wooden plug, poured in river gravel, filling it about a third of the way up from the plug, and then he had plugged above the gravel with another wooden plug that filled the cavity out to the cut end of the bamboo at the handle. As such, it was a weighted sap.

He quickly returned to the scene of the battle. Jordanne wouldn't let go of the bamboo pole, and the fish couldn't get off. It was a tug-of-war that neither was winning. Alec's extra weight and strength turned the tide. In his excitement, he shouted to Jordanne, "Hold this!" handing her the sap and dropping to his knees. Then he seized the line and started line hauling the fish toward the raft. It was a battle royale as he jerked the fish in, only to have it race away as soon as it saw the raft. He had to let go of the line and grab the rod when that happened. He had to stand up to fight the fish with the rod. The tug-of-war began again. Finally, after fifteen minutes of the mad back and forth, the fish began to tire. Alec pulled it against the side of the raft, reached around it with his left arm, and hoisted it aboard. Jordanne instantly began bashing it with the bat, sometimes hitting it and sometimes missing. She also whaled a blow to Alec's thigh for which she yelled "Sorry," but she kept up her attack until her flipping, writhing foe was subdued. Nearly breathless, she continued beating the fish in the head until it was clearly dead of a crushed skull.

"Got it!" she shouted exultantly. Alec sat down and looked at their prize. It was four feet long and weighed nearly fifty pounds. As such, it was the greatest fish they had caught by far.

He held his hand out to her and drew her to him. He raised her arm over her head as she clung to the bat and proclaimed, "You are the champ! You are the Girl Fishing Champeen of this whole damned river!"

"Yahoo!" she yelled. "Let's eat!"

Grinning at each in triumph, they slid into a mooring site, set up camp for the night, and addressed the consumption of some of their conquest. It was everything ballyhooed about it. The cod of the Amazon didn't do it justice. She compared it to halibut. He, stuffing another chunk into his mouth, agreed. Their lovemaking that night set off a great day of joy and happiness. It was their last for some time.

Early the next morning, Alec set about processing and preserving as much of the arapaima as he could. "I hope you don't mind stuffing yourself with your fish," he told her. "We're going to have to eat as much as we can or lose it."

"You cook. I'll gorge," she answered.

It was nearly midday when they finally took to the river. They were rounding a great headland of crumbling limestone that thrust its bare breast out of the surrounding jungle, and around which the river was forced to flow down, southward and to the right. They had just cleared the point when he pointed and said, "Christ Almighty! Look at that."

"What is it?" Jordanne, puzzled, asked even as she gazed at the scene he pointed out.

"A fuckin' gold rush," he answered. "It's already started."

They watched the spectacle as they floated well out in the river clear of the rushing boats driven by outboard motors of every description and age, mostly ancient. They were running full throttle—swerving, sideswiping one another. Some were shooting wildly in the middle of the melee as they tried to gain advantage. There were dozens, leading the rush with more just leaving the listing docks of a village that was sheltered in the lee of the limestone headland.

"How did they find out so soon?" Jordanne wondered.

"That guy that got away from us had to have had a boat. He has been down here for days. Gold is its own messenger. Travels like wildfire. He undoubtedly let it slip where he got our gold. They probably forced it out of him. There is very little honor in gold rushers. This is a macabre way of looking at it, but if we're lucky, they did him in. Besides you and me, he's the only witness to my shooting that bastard partner of his. A lying witness at that."

"My god!" she said, amazed. "Those crazy sons of bitches are going to kill one another before they ever find the gold."

"Oh, yeah," he said, "no doubt some of 'em are going to bite a bullet, but some of 'em are going to come out with fortunes in gold."

"You really aren't thinking 'us,' are you?" she asked.

Before he answered, he ordered, "Get the rifle handy. We've got company coming."

She turned her gaze in the direction of his pointing finger. A small aluminum boat was motoring toward them. She noted two men in the boat—one forward, one aft—handling the outboard. It was off plane, but moving steadily in their direction. "I'll do the talking," Alec said quietly. "But you load a shell in the chamber. You are going to have to be strong. You may have to shoot. If you do, be quick about it. Don't think, just do it. We'll sort out all the shit later. Can you do it?"

"You mean kill someone?"

"Yes, Jordanne! Expect these guys to be up to no good, probably armed, and willing to shoot us if they can get the drop on us. They may know we have gold. Don't rule that out. These guys are dangerous. You have to be more dangerous than they are."

"Alec, I'm scared," she said, her voice close to breaking.

"Good," he said. "Being scared is handy in situations like this. Just be brave too. Here they are."

The boat nosed alongside the raft. The man in the bow had moved back amidships and grabbed the stern cleat on the starboard side of the raft. He pulled the boat even and against the raft. The man handling the motor cut the power, and both parties stared at each, sizing each other up. The only noise was that of the stampede a half mile toward shore, a solid distant roar punctuated by the sharp reports of occasional gunshots. The noise was detached from the attention of the little group eyeballing each other.

"Hola," said the motorman in greeting.

"Howdy," Alec replied. "Something we can help you with?"

"Oh, si" was the response.

"I don't speak Spanish," Alec said. "So speak English."

"Nice raft. Even has the motor slot in the stern. Wouldn't take much to put a motor on it. You build it yourself?"

"I did," Alec said. He was lightly and casually tapping the fish knocker on his right leg. His eyes searched the pair until he spied what he suspected. The speaker was hiding a sidearm. The holster for it strapped to the man's right thigh was empty at the moment. He figured that was why the man's right hand was sheltered behind his leg and rear seat of the boat.

"Would you sell it?"

"Ah, not right now," he said. "It's too far to swim to shore from here."

The fellow laughed. His teeth, an amalgam of rot, tobacco stains, and gaps matched the rest of him. "Say," he followed, "a feller came by this way a few days ago. Had some gold on him. That's why all those crazy bastards over there are in such a hurry. Feller claimed he got it from a guy and a woman up at the mouth of the Rio Estrella. Said they shot his partner. Said they had a lot of gold on 'em. You wouldn't know about that, would you?"

"Naw, I wouldn't know about that. Where is that feller now?"

"Oh, he had a bad accident."

"Yeah, bad accidents are easy to come by out here."

The man turned and pointed with his left hand. "Look at that hoorah over there. Ya think they'll find gold up that river?"

Alec didn't look. Instead, he kept a steady gaze on the hand behind the leg and seat.

"Jordanne?"

"Got him."

Suddenly, the motorman shifted his weight and rapidly swung a pistol to bear on Alec. The gun belched as Alec lunged aside and down. The bullet sailed away across the river. The blast of the rifle behind him was, by comparison, overpowering. The top of the head of the shooter disappeared in a vivid geyser of red. Alec pivoting on the deck and swinging his bat with both hands made solid contact with the head of the second boatman, knocking him across the boat to the opposite gunwale where he bounced and fell to the bottom of the boat. A revolver slipped out of his left hand and rattled against the center seat. Alec quickly grabbed the nearside gunwale of the boat and pulled it against the raft before the two could separate beyond reach. "Jordanne!" he called. "Hand me a rope." When she didn't move, he yelled, "Jordanne! Hand me a rope!"

It took a moment longer, but then she moved with purpose. "What do we do now?" she asked.

"We're throwin' 'em overboard," he said, tying off the boat to the raft.

"But that one isn't dead."

"See that gun right there? The only reason one of us, probably me, isn't dead is because I hit him before he could get his gun up. They came out here to kill us and take our gold, Jordanne. Turnabout in this goddamned hellhole is fair play. For right now, we are in shoot-first country."

Alec stepped into the boat and used an oar that was lying against the port side to shift the boat to the offshore side of the raft. After checking their pockets, he stripped their gun belts. He then pitched the pair into the river. Then he worked for a few minutes and after an awkward bout of heaving and straining, he managed to drag the outboard motor into the boat. He disconnected the fuel tank and set it on the raft. "Here," he instructed her. "Use this oar to keep us positioned so they can't see what we are doing from shore."

"What are you doing?" she asked with emphasis.

"You'll see in a minute. Swing us back around."

When she had them settled, backs to shore, he said, "Kneel down and hold onto the boat." She did as he said, trusting him without question, for once. He set an outboard motor tank on the raft. Then he wallowed the outboard onto the edge of the boat and rolled it onto the raft. He quickly looked the unit over, pleased to see it was an older ten-horse Evinrude.

She couldn't help herself. "What's that for?"

"Escape." He then looked the boat over carefully for anything that could help them. Other than the two handguns, the only item of value left in the boat was a sheath knife that the motorman had lying beside him on his seat. There was no ammunition for either handgun, except for that in the guns themselves. Alec then crossed back onto the raft. He went forward and dug out their fireman's axe.

"What are you going to do now?" she asked.

"Sink the boat."

"Why?"

"Because."

"Because why?

"Because I said so! Keep us ass to the shore, Jordanne," he ordered. "I'll explain when we have time. Right now, I don't."

He stepped back aboard and began swinging the pick of the axe through the thin aluminum bottom of the boat. Water geysered upward and began rapidly filling the small craft. Alec tossed the axe onto the raft and stepped out of the boat onto the raft to watch its progress. It quickly filled to the edge of the gunwales and sank down to the level of the water. There, it rested. "Shit!" he said, "That's what I was afraid of."

"What's the matter?" she asked.

"It isn't going down."

"Why not?"

"Flotation material in the seats. It's put in there so the boat won't sink and drown people."

"What are you going to do about it?"

"Nothing. We're going to get out of here. I'll need your help."

The adrenaline-charged minutes finally overcame her, and she folded into a cross-legged seat on the raft. "My god"—she moaned—"I've killed someone."

He turned from where he was examining the cutout in the stern of their raft. "I'm sorry, honey," he said. He stopped what he was doing and knelt beside her. He didn't take her in his arms. Instead, he spoke quietly and insistently to her. "So have I. It's going to take time just to cope with it. We'll never get over it, and we may have to do it again. We are a long way from getting out of this country in more ways than one. It's going to take all the go-for-it courage we both have, even to survive. Trust me. I'll do everything in my power to get us out, even if it kills me."

He returned to the task at hand. He used the saw edge of the machete to square off the bamboo in the slot. He wrestled the outboard into a position from which he could drop it into the water and tighten the transom bolts. "I need your help now," he said. She crawled to him. "I'm going to wrap the rope around the leg, just below the engine cowling," he said. "I'll need you to hold onto the ends of the rope and help me steady the engine while I tighten the lugs. They aren't going to fit very tight, so we'll leave it roped up and tied off to the cleats on either side. Running this thing without losing it is going to be a bitch. We are also going to need to look for a couple of pieces of flat board as we go. I can use those to tighten down the engine so it won't come off."

Working together, they struggled and spent more time than he wanted, but they finally mounted the old motor on their raft. He was able to get it to fire up, and they moved off at a crippling slow pace, that was, nevertheless, breathtaking at raft speed. "This is a hell of a way to do it," he said, looking at her with happy eyes, "but we are on our way."

Chapter 8

For the rest of that day, they motored well out on the river, closer to the far north bank than the center. They had made no attempt to approach the village from which the gold mad flotilla had sprung. Late in the afternoon, Jordanne had spotted a piece of board they were able to cut and sandwich onto the bamboo stern. The outboard was screwed onto the raft solidly enough for the speed they were able to travel without burying the bow of the raft underwater. The relief that provided Alec was wonderful. All day, they had watched motorboat traffic on the south side moving upriver. None of the boats had detoured to investigate them.

Jordanne began to gradually work her way out of the shock that had struck her upon shooting the man in the boat. Idly, she asked Alec, "Are all those boats gold rushers?"

"I think so," he answered. "There's been foot traffic on the river trail too. All headed upriver."

"What's with that?" she continued. "There isn't enough room on the river for that many."

"That's just the start," he said. "There will be thousands before it's all over."

She stared moodily across the river. "So why didn't any of those boats come over here?" she asked.

"They don't know we have gold."

"I still don't understand how that one guy could start a gold rush, do you?" she said.

"Well, let me guess. Mr. Runforit goes into the local watering hole and rolls a gold nugget onto the bar. For a free drink, he tells a wild tale about a river upstream that is loaded with gold nuggets just like that one right there. Before long after buying him free drinks, they get it out of him that it's the Rio Estrella. That's our river. Star River. And before the night is over, the rush is on, and Mr. Runforit is too drunk to know what the hell is happening. He is, however, detained out back where his story is plumbed in depth. He spills his guts about a pair of pilgrims, a man and a woman, who have a backpack full of gold. Then he is rolled for his gold, and then he really does spill his guts."

"Hmmm. What about his pal?"

"Big hole in the story. I don't know. Hopefully, that topic didn't come up before Mr. Runforit announced his cold-blooded murder. I wouldn't want to be the subject of a manhunt."

"Please tell me we aren't going back," she pleaded.

He looked forlornly far away up the river. "After today, I don't see much hope for that," he said. "We have to get out of this country. That's proving to be a bloody business."

Suddenly, Jordanne was overcome, "Oh my god!" She wailed. "I killed a man, and we pitched another man into the river to drown. We killed him in cold blood. Drowned him! They're gonna be man hunting me too!"

"No! Jordanne, we didn't kill him in cold blood! He was trying to shoot me," Jones fired back. "He was already dead when I pitched him into the river. I crushed his skull when I hit him with the bat. So stop! Just stop with the drama! I don't like what we've done either, but what would have happened if we hadn't? We didn't initiate any of this, and every one of those men shot at us, or would have. So get real! Stop wasting your tears on murderous scumbags. Feel bad. But get over it for now." She sobbed for a little longer, but finally wiped her nose and looked to help him with the raft.

It was nearly dusk when they spotted a little cove on the north side of the river. They beached the raft, set the anchor, and built a small fire to cook another dinner of the arapaima. It was excellent, but both were silently thinking of salt and other protein. "You know, I wonder what the natives are eating over there on the other side of the river," Jordanne said to the air as much as to Alec.

"Tacos," he said.

"Just shut up!" she squealed. "I'd eat half of that raft for a taco."

"God, I wish I hadn't said that! I'd eat the other half for one myself."

"Is there any chance we can stop in one of those villages we keep passing?" she asked, looking at him hopefully.

"Well, things are improving. Before we killed them, we did find someone who could speak English."

They continued motoring downriver for two days before daring to start checking out the settlements along the river. On the morning of the third day, they again bound Jordanne, and she put her hair up. They chose a village that they thought looked more prosperous. Its docks weren't sagging, and it had a broad beach beside a launch where they could beach the raft. The small collection of huts formed a plaza of sorts. From there, they could watch the raft. They both wore a gun strapped to their sides. They blended right in, except for their color and race. They strolled around, listening for any words of English and hoping someone would get curious and come speak to them. The best they were able to do was smile, smile, smile. They watched tortillas being made. Jordanne asked quietly in a whisper in an aside, "How do we pay for any of this? Do you have any money?"

"Not a cent."

"Any ideas?"

"Barter."

"Barter what?"

He grinned. "How gamey are you feeling?"

"Oh for Chrissake!" she blurted. Several of the people heard her.

One of them timidly approached. She was a young woman trailing two children behind her. "Padre?" she asked.

Alec spoke to her as he had in the other village far upriver. "*No hablo Español. ¿Tu hablo Inglés?*"

She smiled eagerly and repeated "Padre" in the affirmative.

He turned and said to Jordanne, "Look, I think we are in luck here. If I understand her, there is a priest around here who speaks English. Can you look after the raft while I go with her to find this guy?"

"Is there some way to send for him?"

"Don't think so. There she goes. She's waving for me to come along. My entire vocabulary has been spent. I'll be right back."

Jordanne, moving unobtrusively and trying to walk manlike, eased back and stepped up on the raft. There she sat down with her knees raised. She casually sat and re-sat until she was able to get the rifle positioned where she could bring it into play if trouble were to manifest itself. She pulled the backpack out and used it for a seat. Finally satisfied, she settled down to wait.

Alec followed the native woman. She led him to a small church built up against the hillside about a hundred yards from the plaza. She crossed herself, genuflected in the entryway and entered the dark interior. Straight ahead, down a center aisle, stood the altar. On the wall behind it was a large crucifix. The woman called for Padre Esteban. Shortly, a pudgy black-robed man of the cloth emerged from a side door. He spoke to her in Spanish. She replied, and he turned to take in Alec, who stood with his hat in his hand. "I am Father Esteban. Sophia tells me you seek him who speaks English," he said in a rich baritone one would have expected from someone of taller and grander stature.

"She is correct, Father. I need to speak to someone in the worst way."

"Very well," the priest said. He turned to the woman and spoke to her rapidly in Spanish. She smiled and walked past Alec back toward the front.

As she passed him, Alec said, "*Mucho gracias.*" Then he turned to the priest, thinking quickly about how much he could reveal. "I am Alec Jones, Father."

"Are you here for confession?" the padre asked.

"No. I'm traveling downriver. I am in the company of another. We are both Americans, and the only two survivors of a plane crash on the ridges above Rio Estrella. I have built a raft, and we have acquired a small motor to push it. What I need is information about where I am and how far it is to some place where I can make connections to get back to the United States and some food to supply us to where we can resupply."

The priest looked at him thoughtfully. "There is a gold strike on the Rio Estrella, and many murders are reported already. The sinful greed for gold makes men go mad. You had to come down the Rio Estrella to get onto this river. You have come a very long way, but you have a very, very long way to go by raft. Three hundred river miles, perhaps more. You are getting into country controlled by drug cartels. There is an American consulate in El San Sabo. There, you can reach your contacts in America. As for food, do you have any money?"

"No."

"Do you have gold?"

"No."

"Have you anything to barter?"

Alec unbuckled his gun belt and handed it and the pistol to the priest. He accepted it and spun the cylinder, noticing a fired cartridge. "This is a very expensive gun," he commented. "It is worth much more than you can get for it here in this poor village." He handed the belt and gun back. "There is a much larger village downriver. You will have to bypass two poorer villages to reach it, but it has become much richer because of the drug traffickers. There, I recommend you trade your gun and belt, along with your raft, for a motorboat. With a good motor, you will stand a chance to slip past the patrols if you travel at night. At times, you will need the speed of a good motor that can put your boat on plane so you can run for the reeds to hide. You will need to stock up on extra fuel, at least two extra tanks. Three would be better. Pack a week's worth of food. Supplement it with fishing. Toward the mouth of the river, it starts to braid as it slows down. You must watch for the current. Stay with it like a hound on a scent. When the tide comes in, the river flows backward. You will have to wait till it turns. El San Sabo is situated on the coast on the north bank of the river. For now, come with me."

The priest led Alec back to the plaza. Jordanne saw them coming. She met them in the plaza, where Alec had spoken to the native woman. "Hey, Dan," Alec said, "do you have anything, anything at all, you can barter for food?"

Jordanne looked at him as if he couldn't be serious. She shrugged and reached into her hip pocket. She pulled out the shard of mirror. She had taped the edges with adhesive tape. She handed it to Alec. He looked at himself, grunted, and turned to the priest. He too looked at himself before turning to one of the people making tortillas. He spoke to the man and showed him the mirror. The man took the mirror and held it up to his face. He looked surprised at the image looking back at him. He wrinkled his nose, and the image wrinkled back. He laughed at himself. Then he spoke to the priest.

"What do you want for the mirror?" the priest asked. "Ask for much more than you figure it's worth. To do less would insult him. The people love to haggle."

Alec shot the moon. "Ten pounds of flour, ten pounds of beans, five pounds of salt, and three pounds of potatoes, and two pounds of red chili peppers. And two tortillas."

The priest smiled gleefully and laid it on the man. There was what appeared an angry outburst, and the man waved his arms while looking disgustedly at Alec. Then in Spanish, he spoke at length to Father Esteban. He translated, "You are like a dog that eats its young. Have you no pride? How can you live with yourself trying to rob a poor man? He offers two pounds of flower, two pounds of beans, one pound of salt, one pound of potatoes, and one pound of chili peppers."

Alec, getting into the swing of the haggle, sadly shook his head. "Tell him he will be the envy of every man and woman in the village. He can sell looks in the mirror for many months, if not years. Tell him I am only a poor traveler, very much like himself. I cannot accept his offer. Tell him seven pounds of flour and beans, two pounds of salt, three pounds of potatoes, and one pound of chili peppers. And two tortillas."

The barter continued until the priest said, "Done!" The final tally was five pounds of flour, three pounds of beans, one pound of salt, two pounds of potatoes, and one pound of chili peppers. And two tortillas. All of it, except the tortillas was packed in cloth bags and tied off with wire. Alec and Jordanne carried it to the raft and tucked it inside the sleeping hut. After devouring the tortillas, they prepared to depart. The priest called Alec to the side for a final private conference. "You have a beautiful raft," he said. "Don't part with it cheaply. On this river, such a raft has great value. When you reach the village of which I spoke, go to the chapel of the Holy Cross. There, ask for Father Sebastian. He will convert some of your gold into pesos." Alec started to interrupt. The priest waved him off. "Do not protest. I knew of you before your appearance. I do not cast the first stone. At some time, you must make peace with God. As for now, I wish you safe journeys, and may God bestow his blessings upon you. I will pray for you. Goodbye, my son." He turned and began walking back into the plaza.

On impulse, Alec called a question to the departing priest, "Father, what is the name of this river?"

"It is aptly named. It is Rio El Diablo."

The rest of the day was spent marveling at their good fortune. "That tortilla was the food of the gods!" Jordanne enthused. She lay flat on her back, watching clouds float by and intermingle. She looked for shapes, animals, and faces. "We need to name the raft," she announced.

Alec had been quiet, brooding. "Yeah. Go ahead."

"Don't you have a name to suggest?"

"No, I haven't given it a thought. Wouldn't have one if I did."

"Why?"

"Because, in a couple of days, we are trading it in on a boat."

"On a boat? We had a boat, remember? And now you want another one? Don't tell me you plan to sink it too!"

"That boat would have been recognized. It would have been, on this river, like driving a hot Lamborghini, through downtown Phoenix. I spoke to the priest about what we are up against. He laid it out plain enough. We are up shit creek."

"He didn't say that, did he?"

"No, but I lied about the gold, and there at the last, he called me on it. Said he knew who I was before I met him. That's got me spooked. He knows my name, but he doesn't know yours. He says to go to the chapel of the Holy Cross in this village we're headed to. A priest named Father Sebastian will exchange some of our gold for pesos. We are going to need money to get out of here, sweetheart. The priest is going to pray for us. Wouldn't be a bad idea to offer some of our own."

For the better part of two days, they continued downriver on the north shore side. Alec kept a sharp eye out for the two villages the priest had spoken to him about. He was also jumpy and moody at the same time. Jordanne tried to cheer him up to no avail. Finally, she became angry. "What the hell's up with you?" she demanded.

"Nothing's up with me."

"Oh, bullshit," she countered. "I know you well enough to know that. You have been moping around for the past two days, ever since you talked to that priest. What the hell's bugging you?"

"Yeah, you're right. What's bugging me is lying to that priest. That bothered me, but when he caught me at it, that really got to me."

She looked at him, thoughtfully. "I can see that. You've killed two men and lied to a priest. Has to be preying on your conscience. But to quote someone I heard in the recent past, we are in a lawless land, here, with gold that every son of a bitch on the river is willing to kill us for. Some have already tried it. Some, we probably have yet to kill. This is survival. Its dog eat dog. It's going to take both of us working together and concentrating on the immediate: what we can control. Compartmentalize. No drama. Get over it." She paused before she got into a rant. Then she shouted. "Get over it, Alec! I can't make it if you don't hang onto your strength. You are our salvation here. If you piss away into melancholy, we're doomed."

He was startled at the vehemence of her outburst. He shook his head. "You're right. Okay. I'm back. Come here." She stepped back to where he sat on the backpack handling the motor. "Kiss me, you fool," he said. She complied eagerly. They sat together for a long time and watched the second village disappear around a bend in the river.

That night, they ate a rough sort of tortilla. Neither was an accomplished cook, so their dough was lumpy with dry flour blisters, and some of the ingredients were a bit raw. They had been soaking their beans too long, so they were mushy, but the break from eating fish, even with salt, was gratefully received. For the first time in a while, they lay in conjugal bliss on the deck. They enjoyed stargazing and talking about small things. When they decided to turn in, they found that ferns they had chopped earlier in the day to try for bedding instead of boughs were softer. They both slept well and woke the next morning refreshed. After a quick breakfast of leftover tortilla, they weighed anchor and pulled out into the river. "I hope to hell we find that village today," Alec groused as they set off. "We're about out of fuel."

The village, when they found it the next day, was a sharp contrast to anything they had seen before. People were busy bustling around with purpose. There were actual streets with donkey carts loaded with wood, produce, and fish delivering to different establishments and plazas. The population was several thousand, and as a result, the village sprawled over two- or three-square miles. The docks were busy with watercraft of varying sizes moving in and out. Alec looked for a place to beach the raft, motoring along slowly. Finally, Jordanne pointed to an open area beyond the last dock. "How about there?"

He looked to where she pointed. It was hard against jungle that grew to the edge of the river. He didn't like it, but there was no other place where they could beach a raft. After setting out the anchor, they discussed how to go about finding the chapel of the Holy Cross. Jordanne was once again bound flat with her hair stringing out around under the brim of her hat. She looked like an overgrown tomboy.

"Do you feel like you can guard the raft while I go look?" Alec asked hopefully.

"Not a chance. You could be gone for hours. In this place, I'd either get killed in a shootout or kidnapped and stuck in a whorehouse. Where you go, I go."

"Well, we'll probably lose the raft then," he said huffily.

"What would you rather lose, me or the raft?"

Alec looked at her lamely. "You got any ideas on how to keep the raft?"

She looked at him doubtfully. "Me? You're asking me? Isn't that a little more in your job description? But if you want my opinion, forget about the raft. We have half a million in gold in that backpack. Just enough cash to buy a boat and not worry about haggling while trying to trade in a raft. How the hell are you going to do that anyway? You don't even speak the language."

He stood forlornly staring at his raft. "She's a beautiful raft," he said. "The first time I ever built something like that so well. But as much as I hate to say it, you're right."

They loaded the backpack, exchanging the fire axe for the fish bat. She strapped on the machete over her gun belt. He wore his gun belt, shouldered the backpack, and carried the rifle. He took one last look at his beautiful raft. "The priest said a raft like mine is worth a lot of money on this river. I just hope the next owner appreciates it as much as I did."

They trudged up into the village, sticking out like a man of the cloth in a house of ill repute. They drew stares from all they passed. They smiled and nodded pleasantly. None were returned. "Suspicious sorts, aren't they?" She observed.

"Suspicious, hell," he responded. "Hostile is more like it. You're from Phoenix, lots of Spanish influence. Are there any churches there with cross in their names?"

"No, the only thing I can think of is a town in New Mexico called Las Cruces. I think it means the cross, or something like that."

"Okay, we'll go with that. Let's start asking for Las Cruces."

They felt like fools or even idiots, as anyone who has ever been in a foreign land with no way to communicate feels, but they kept at it. "My god"—Jordanne groaned—"I'm smiling because my face is too cramped to stop."

No one would listen without turning silently away until a child pointed toward a hill that sloped off the main ridge. Before Alec could say gracias, the child had fled.

"Let's go that way," he said. As they walked, the path gradually rose until they could look down upon the waterfront. He paused to rest and pointed to the spot where they had beached their raft. It was gone.

"They don't waste time in these parts, do they?" she said.

They kept walking until they crested the lower slope of the ridge the child had pointed to. The chapel was tucked against the backdrop of the jungle that blanketed the hills that folded one into another along the line of ridges, fading into the blue distance far upriver. "There it is, isn't it?" Jordanne asked excitedly.

"It's got to be," he said. "There can't be more than one Catholic church in a village out here, no matter what size the place is."

As they approached the church, Alec spoke to Jordanne, "Sweetheart," he said, "we're going to have to trust these people. You can't wear a hat into the chapel. That is a sacrilege they don't tolerate."

"Then why don't I wait outside?"

"Because these churches are refuges. Not even the cartels will violate a church. We are likely to be here awhile, a day or so. You'll be all right in here."

"Yeah, but what if they don't trust us?"

"We'll buy some," he said.

Their entrance into the church was seen nearly as soon as it was made. A slender robed figure met them as they were approaching the altar. He, apparently noting by their appearance that they were Anglo, asked in perfectly unaccented English, "May I help you?"

Alec, hat in hand, said, "We are here at the instruction of Father Esteban to ask for Father Sebastian."

"He is not in at present. Can you wait?"

"Yes."

With that, the padre indicated the front pews to them and disappeared through a side door.

"Well," Alec said, "we might as well get as comfortable as we can. Church pews aren't quite as uncomfortable as picket fences, but they aren't far behind."

Jordanne removed the machete and gun belt. She handed the gun to Alec. "Here, boy, take care of my gat," she said, folding her gun belt into a makeshift pillow. She stretched out full length. "Wake me when it's over."

Alec looked at her and smiled. He shook his head and muttered, "You!"

They waited for an hour or so when a different robed figure approached them by way of the side door. "You would be Alec Jones," he said. "I am Father Sebastian. How may I help you?"

"Father Sebastian, this is my partner, Jordanne Austin. We are the sole survivors of a plane crash above the Rio Estrella. We are traveling downriver to El San Sabo, where we hope to make connections to return to the United States. Father Esteban assured me that you could assist us."

"I have heard that a raft with two people on board has been coming downriver. The raft was powered by an outboard engine, so it was not a native's raft. They do not do that. There is also a report of two men and a small boat missing from a village above that of Father Esteban. The boat was found sabotaged, but neither man was found. That's to be expected as our crocodiles and caiman are very good at cleaning up carrion in the river. Another rumor has it that the couple is carrying a backpack filled with gold. Do you know of these things?"

"Father," Alec said, cautioning a clearly consternated Jordanne to settle down, "does your church accept donations?"

"Yes. Under some circumstances, however, they are declined."

Alec zipped open the top of the backpack and withdrew the cotton bag that had recently held chili peppers. It was half filled with their gold. "Father, this is gold from the Rio Estrella. We placer mined it ourselves. We came by it honestly. Whatever you may have heard, we have attacked no one. Please accept this donation to your church on our behalf."

The priest looked at the pouch as Alec held it out to him. Jordanne watched in fascinated trepidation as Father Sebastian made no move to accept the offering. Alec continued to silently hold the offering in his extended hand. The seconds seemed to drone on like minutes before the priest finally reached a hand and accepted the offer. Without giving away that he had read the surprise in the priest's face at the weight of the bag, Alec inwardly heaved a sigh of relief.

"How may I assist you?" asked the good father.

"We need a small vee hulled aluminum boat of about twelve feet. A ten to fifteen-horse motor, Evinrude, Johnson, or Mercury, preferred. Three extra tanks of fuel, premixed. A pair of oars, and a good-all-weather dark-green tarp if possible. Netting to protect against flying insects. A pair of strong flashlights. A pair of good ten power binoculars, and food for five days. We would also request some currency to take with us. The amount needed to assist us in making our way to El San Sabo."

"These things will be, anonymously, available to you at dawn tomorrow at the first upstream dock. As theft occurs here very quickly, do not wait until dawn breaks. Be waiting for it. Give me a moment, please."

With that, the priest strode quickly out the side door of the chapel. Presently, he returned and handed Alec a plump leather handbag, much like a woman's small purse. "There is a currency conversion table in this bag," he said. "Go with God." He turned on his heel and left once more through the side door.

Alec handed the money purse to Jordanne as he shrugged into the backpack. "I'll be glad to put this thing back in a boat," he growled.

"How much gold did we donate?" she asked, riffling through a thick packet of bills stuffed into the purse.

"Well, I didn't have a scale, but by heft standards, I would say roundabout two and a half, maybe three pounds."

"So, by heft, at twelve ounces to the pound, that's roundabout thirty ounces times about two thousand dollars, so that's roundabout sixty thousand dollars. Down here in this economy, that's probably, by heft, roundabout a hundred grand. Nice. Very nice. If we weren't standing in a church, I'd give you a big old sloppy kiss 'cuz you bought us some very nice trust."

"I hope so," he said. "Let's go shopping. There are things we are needing."

They returned to the heart of the village and found a booth of sorts with a small table where they could eat. Both ordered tortillas, the only item on the menu, and chased it down with small shots of tequila. Curious, as always, Jordanne wanted to know why the tequila. "The water may not be boiled," Alec told her. "If it isn't, you can expect a case of violent diarrhea bordering on dysentery. You don't want that!"

"Mother of God! How many more ways of killing us does this country have?"

"Let me count the ways. Oh, wait! That goes with loving you. They are about the same. Five hundred."

"Smart-ass," she responded. "Let's go shopping. I'm feelin' tough!"

From the ersatz café, Alec began searching for a sign that indicated guns. After a short search, he found a small shop with a sign painted crudely with the term, ARMA, in capital letters. "Here we go," he said.

"What are we looking for?"

"Ammo," he said. "Lots of ammo."

"Besides shooting scumbags and lying to priests, what other natural abilities do you have?"

"Har dee ho, har, har!" he replied. "Raft building."

Inside the shop, they began looking for ammunition. The calibers they sought were not stocked on the short shelf of boxes of mostly twenty-two calibers. "Let's look at that conversion table the priest told us about," he said. Jordanne pulled it out of the purse.

They both studied the chart. After puzzling a bit, they figured out that a hundred-thousand-peso note was the equivalent of twenty-five US dollars. They looked at their wad and were relieved to see many hundred-thousand-peso notes, along with rich denominations of ten-, twenty-, and fifty-thousand-peso notes. Lesser denominations were also included. Armed with a rudimentary sense of money value, they approached the counter, where a tall angular Colombian stood, smoking a cigarette. "Help you?" he asked.

"You speak English," Alec said vastly relieved. "We need four boxes of nine-millimeter and a box of thirty ought six, and a string and patches for cleaning a rifle if you have it."

"That's a mighty big order for here," the man said. "You need, or you want?"

"Well, that's a matter of circumstance," Alec said. "If you need it and don't have it, then wanting it is really needing it. Either way you look at it, we're buyers."

The man chuckled. "Never heard it put that way before, but it rings true. Funny thing, I can sell you a box of the rifle shells, but only two boxes of the nine. Hate to put a limit on it, but the cartel guys come in here from time to time, and all they shoot is nine mil. Have to have it on hand. I'll have to have four hundred thousand for the three boxes. I'll throw in the cleaning supplies."

Alec turned to Jordanne. "That'll be four big ones," he said.

"Coming right up," she said, turning her back and drawing out four hundred-thousand-peso notes. "Here you go," she said.

The Colombian looked at her and said, "You are a mite old not to have had your voice change, aren't you?" he observed.

She turned away as Alec stepped to shield her from questions. "Thanks for the ammo," he said. The odd pair turned to the door and left.

"You didn't even try to haggle," she said. "And now it isn't bad enough to have to wear my hair under a hat, so I look like a modern-day Tom Sawyer, plus being permanently pressed in a mammogram state, I have to go through the change and lose my boy's voice. Do you have any idea how I hate this country?"

"I'm getting the message," he said. "But you don't haggle with guys who speak English. They just tell you to go get fucked. Let's go find some food, some new duds, and a place to spend the night. We'll sleep on the floor, but at least we'll have a roof over our heads. It's going to rain this afternoon. It always does when it gets that dark out to the west. We need to get a move on and get some fresh clothing. Too bad, Tom. You will have to dress like the man you are!"

"Alright, smart-ass. No frilly come-hither garb for you to ogle either. It's canvas and sandpaper. Try jumping that! And why can't we sleep on the bed?"

"Bed bugs. And for this one, you'll need your hair down. In this country, two guys sharing a bedroom is frowned on."

After finding clothing in a booth off the city's main plaza, they began the search for a suitable place to spend the night. They searched for a hotel down toward the river but had to settle for something more to the center of the village. Alec didn't like it. He was hoping to be able to slip out to the dock just before dawn without being noticed. That hope was dashed as they were a good five or six blocks from the dock where they were to take possession of their boat. The only consolation was that they were at least on the ground floor. As soon as they checked in, they proceeded to their room. Alec took the only chair in the room and jammed it under the doorknob. "Let me show you something," he said. He went to the bed and began lifting the mattress. "Look," he said. The rails of the bed were swarming with small beetle-like bugs. "They're all bloodsuckers and are likely to carry disease as well. Best to let sleeping bugs lie."

Jordanne felt her skin crawl. "I get to sleep next to the wall," she said. "How about the pillows? Are they bug ridden as well?"

"Let's look," he said. He pulled one off the bed and jerked it out of the pillowcase. Then he peeled the seams open and peered carefully into the stitching. He was patient and thorough, examining minutely, his nose nearly touching the pillow.

"What are you looking for?" she asked, puzzled.

"Nits."

"What are nits?"

"Eggs. They are tiny damned near impossible to see. There," he said, "all done. We'll turn the pillowcase inside out and use that pillow as soon as I have scorched the seams to burn up any I might not have seen." He repeated the process with the other pillow and pronounced it fit to use as soon as he completed the same process. Next, he turned his attention to their guns. He was surprised and pleased to find some Rem Oil in a tube had been included. Jordanne watched him and snuggled next to him.

"Can I help?" she asked.

He smiled, kissed her, and said, "Sure can. But I forgot something. We can untie your bindings. Let's do that first. From now on, you are going to be you. Our cat is out of the bag. We're running naked, babe, from here on out." After cleaning and oiling their guns, they enjoyed the evening in connubial bliss, highlighted by Jordanne's delight with having a pillow. They redressed and slept in their clothes. The warmth was appreciated, and Alec wanted no delay in getting out and down to the river the following morning.

It was well after midnight when they crept as quietly as they could from their room. The lobby of the small hotel was empty. There was no night clerk. They found their way to the river from the reflected light off the water. Alec found an alley corner they could shelter behind from which they could watch the dock. Their dock was directly below them, and he was able to see the entirety of all the docks and areas surrounding them. He watched for the silent approach of boats and men and the sudden flitting of moving shadows.

"Do they have bounties out on us," Jordanne whispered.

"No," he whispered back to her. "No one would pay to put a bounty on the scumbags that tried to kill us. As far as they're concerned, those guys got what they deserved. Why would anyone be concerned with bounties on us when we have a backpack full of gold?"

"But how did they find out about it?"

"Rumor and gold, both are lightning quick. We haven't exactly been moving at light speed. That's why I said our cat's out of the bag. Every person, including the priests, have known about us days before we landed any place. The only reason we haven't been attacked is because they are afraid we'll shoot upon their approach. Our reputation is no secret. Four missing men will do that. From here on out, we are going to shoot first because we have more than one kind of gold with us."

"What do you mean by that?" she continued, whispering.

"You."

"Me!" she exclaimed aloud.

"Shhh!" He shushed her. "Yes, you. A blonde like you, as a call girl down here, is priceless. Not in a two-bit whorehouse. You would never be wasted there. You would be a very high-priced play toy for the guests of a cartel, whichever cartel grabbed you."

"What if I refused?"

"Oh, you would. For whatever that's worth. You would be beaten like a horse until your spirit is broken."

"Dear God, get me out of here!"

"Trying," he said.

They waited for another hour before dawn's earliest light began sifting along the quietly flowing water and onto land. The arrival of the boat came via a man poling the craft up to the dock and tying it off. He crouched down on the dock, seemingly waiting for them. "Come on," Alec said, "let's go." They moved out, staying low and hustling. When they reached the dock and hurried to the boat, the ferryman held the boat against the dock while they clambered aboard.

Then he spoke in English, "Use the pole to get yourself out into the river. Try to get downstream around the next bend in the river before you start the motor. You are supposed to be watched, but you may be ahead of the spies. Time will tell. Good luck." As he started to push them away from the dock, Alec caught his arm and pressed four one-hundred-thousand-peso notes into his hand. The man glanced at the money and smiled. "Like I said, good luck. When you power up, stay close to the north side and go like hell." He then moved quickly away up the dock and out of sight.

"How much did you tip him?" Jordanne asked.

"Four hundred."

"Why so much?"

"Goodwill. He is much less likely now to turn us over. If he wanted, he could put the dogs on us within the hour. He might anyway, in time, but he is more than likely to say nothing until he has to. That could give us several hours head start."

Alec poled them out into the current, then affixed the oarlocks, and began rowing them downriver as swiftly as he could. A half hour later, the village was out of sight, around a gently left turning bend of the river. Alec decided to check out the boat and motor. The boat was a high-sided twelve-footer in used but in sturdy condition. There was only one tank that could be pressurized, but there were three additional five-gallon Jerry cans of fuel lined up, side by side between the rear and middle seats, and secured with line to the starboard oarlock. "Let's see if the rest of our stuff is here," he called to Jordanne.

"We should have a black or green tarp, netting, flashlights a pair of binoculars, and food. How did we do?"

"Where would I look?" she asked.

"Up there, under the deck."

Presently, she turned around and gave him a thumbs up. "All here," she said.

Alec assessed the engine. It was a Johnson fifteen horse. He had been hoping for a ten. Fuel consumption was a primary concern, and he felt, from his experience, that a ten horse would get them a lot farther downriver than a fifteen horse. When he stopped to assess the situation, however, he had to admit to himself that they would probably have to stop somewhere for fuel. If all they had to do was to move at trolling speed, he was sure they could putt-putt it to the coast. On plane was a different proposition. He squeezed the primer bulb until it was tight, pulled the choke, and ripped the starting cord. After four pulls, the engine came smoothly to life. He pushed the choke back in, pushed the shifting arm into forward, and twisted the throttle for speed. The boat moved out nicely, and he called to Jordanne to get ready to rock and roll. He moved the throttle smoothly to full; the boat came up on plane, and they were moving at close to thirty-five miles an hour. It seemed like a hundred. He looked at Jordanne. She was clearly frightened as she knelt in the bottom of the boat with her chin tucked. She had stuffed her hat into the backpack, so her hair swirled in a mass about her head and shoulders despite the effect of a small deflection screen mounted across the small deck that enclosed four feet of the bow. He didn't care, the words of the ferryman echoed in his brain. "Go like hell."

For the next two hours, Alec kept the relentless pace. He finally dropped speed when he saw a shallow point reaching out into the river. Jordanne looked up. "What's happening?" she asked.

"Piss stop," he said. He nosed the boat into the shallow water, and then turned and popped the engine into the up position. "Damn!" he said," I didn't ask for an anchor." He waited until the boat nosed into the gravel bar. It struck suddenly and held fast. Jordanne stood up on wobbly legs, reached unsteadily for the gunwale of the boat, and clumsily stepped on land. There she stood, weaving a bit, trying to get her bearings. Alec was busy rooting about under the cover of the deck. "Aha!" he exclaimed, looking triumphantly at her. "Look what I found."

"Congratulations. You found an anchor and some rope."

"Don't knock it," he said. "This is a game changer. Suddenly, I love that priest."

"You're even then. He loves your money."

"Don't be snide. This boat came pretty well equipped."

"As long as it gets us there. Just don't fall in love with it. We are probably going to abandon it, just like we did the raft. How far do you think we've come?"

"Sixty miles or so."

"How far do we have left to go?"

"Not sure. If I had to guess, I'd put it at around three hundred miles. I don't think any further than that though."

"How long is that going to take?"

"That, my dear, is the sixty-four-dollar question."

"It seemed to me like we were going like a bat out of hell."

"We were for a twelve-foot boat. Probably thirty, thirty-five miles an hour. But the boys from the cartels have speed boats that can do seventy to eighty, or more if they want to."

"I didn't see any of those at that marina."

"And you won't either," he said. *"They have private marinas, with heliports, and hot-and-cold running women."*

She shuddered. "Let's piss and get going."

Chapter 9

Alec maintained their breakneck pace for the next several hours, always hugging the north side of the river. He had suggested to Jordanne that she sit up on the seat and look around to avoid the queavies when they stopped. He sat to the left of the engine to operate the throttle with his right hand, so he positioned her to the right, or starboard side of the boat, to balance out the load. He kept a weather eye ahead, behind, and toward the south side of the river. It was nearing midmorning when he spotted another stream flowing into their river from the north. He throttled down and began motoring toward its mouth. Jordanne looked startled as soon as he dropped power, and when the engine noise was subdued enough to talk over, she asked loudly, "What are we doing now?"

"Exploring."

"Why?"

"Look back there."

She gazed back up the river, even shading her eyes with her hands. "Are those little white plumes boats?" she asked.

"They are. Moving fast too. Probably fifty, maybe fifty-five, miles an hour."

"I thought you said they drove seventy."

"They can if they want to, but those cartel boys have the same problem we do. Fuel. And they have to turn around and go back. That's our advantage. We're going to hide out until we see them head back upriver. That's why we're gonna duck in here and hide until we see them head back. We'll take turns watching with the binoculars. Then, sweetheart, we are going to go putt-putt all night. If you are tired, this would be a good time to get some sleep."

Alec cruised up the side river, looking for a place to pull in. He wanted to stay low down in the mouth so they could watch the Rio El Diablo for the return of the speedboats. Fortunately, there was a small gravel bar on the east shore. He powered at it, cut the motor with the stop switch, and popped the engine into the up position. "Hang on, Jordanne!" he yelled. The boat nosed up onto the bar but came to a sudden stop. She didn't. As she was thrown forward, she ducked and plowed headfirst under the deck. He rushed forward to help her extricate herself. She came up swinging. "You bastard, you!" she shrieked. "You could have given me some warning. You could have killed me!"

He was laughing as he caught her wildly swinging arms and pulled her to him. "I'm sorry." He laughed harder." Oh, Jesus, you should have seen your ass stuck up in the air like that. You looked like a bear in a badger hole." He couldn't help himself and kept laughing for a few more minutes. Then he helped her look for scrapes and knicks. Except for a scuff to an elbow that didn't draw blood, she was fine. It took her half an hour to finally run through her adrenaline.

"You wait," she finally said. "You're gonna get yours. You just mark my words."

Alec walked around in the trees until he found a spot from which to scan the big river with the binoculars. He combed the far shore for fifteen or twenty minutes. Thinking to call to Jordanne to take a turn, he turned around to find her crouched three feet behind him. She screeched at the top of her voice and jumped at him. He jerked backward with a cry of alarm—stumbled, tripped, and dropped onto his tailbone. She laughed and pointed at him. "Gotcha!" He groveled in pain. When he tried to sit up, he couldn't. At first, she laughed some more, but as it became apparent that he was injured in some way, she became frightened. "What did you do?" she cried.

"Tailbone," he groaned. "Hit a rock or something. Can't move my legs."

"Can't move your legs! Oh, Christ, what did I do? I didn't mean to. I'm so sorry!"

"Jordanne, what's done is done! We have to get over it, and right now, I'm going to need a walking stick. Go get the machete and find something about as thick as your wrist and as tall you are. I'm going to see if I can get some feeling into my legs."

Jordanne stood staring, her face turning white. "I didn't mean to hurt you." She sobbed brokenly as the possibility of his potential disability struck her.

He looked at her, pain twisting his face into a grimace. "It's not all your fault. If I hadn't laughed at you, you wouldn't have wanted to get even. We just got unlucky is all. Sweetheart. Please, Jordanne, go see if you can find me a walking stick."

She turned and moved away on unsteady legs, frightening possibilities beginning to force their way into her mind. Numbly, she searched until she found the machete. With something to do, she began to process the situation. As she searched, she began thinking through what she would have to do if Alec were to be laid up, even short-term. Food preparation, running the boat, aiding Alec as he tried to get around. Toilet functions! Tears began flowing in earnest. She eventually settled on cutting a section of bamboo. She ran back to where Alec was sitting, heaved over to one side off his tailbone. "How are you doing?" she asked anxiously.

"Better," he said. "Hurts like hell every time I move, but I can feel my legs. There, for just a second, I thought I might be paralyzed. This ain't good, but it ain't paralysis either. Oh, good! You got me a walking stick. I'll need your help to get up." Then began a rather colossal struggle to erect him to his feet. His bellowing nearly unnerved her as they wrestled, wallowed, and rolled until he figured out what he could and couldn't do. At last, their exertions had her standing on his left, supporting him while he clung to the bamboo with his right hand. Sweat poured off both of them as they rested, waiting for him to gather the nerve to take a first step. He took a small step forward with his right leg and collapsed. He howled like a wild thing as he rolled to his left off his right side.

Jordanne began to panic. He yelled at her, "Stop it! You aren't going to do us any good doing that. I know where the injury is now. On the right. I'll be all right leading left and trailing right. Now, help me get back up." Once more the exertions began, but shortly they had him standing with the walking stick in his left hand and her supporting the right. Cautiously, he led with a small left step. It held. He dragged his right to follow. Very slowly, they crept back to the boat.

"What now?" she asked as they stood swaying and looking around at the small clearing that fronted the side river before them. He spotted a tree at the far edge.

"Let's see if we can get to that big tree over there where I can sit with my back to it."

When he was finally positioned in a sitting position on his left hip, he took a few moments to rest, leaning his head back against the tree trunk. He looked at her, assessing how she was holding up. It was unclear, so he began building her up. "God, what a relief," he said. "Could never have done it without you. You were great: got me a walking stick, raised me to my feet, packed me over here and sat me down. Thanks, sweetheart. Without you, I would be toast right now."

She perked up. "What are we gonna do now?"

"Set up camp. Take another look tomorrow. This blow to my ass is going to take some rest. I'm shot for today."

"All right. What do I need to do?"

"I have a sneaking feeling we need to hide our gold. If the cartel boys, or treasure hunters, find us, we don't want that gold anywhere near us. Without that, the incentive to do us in would be a lot less. Just needless cold-blooded murder is still taken seriously, even here. I suspect our presence on the river has even been noted at the American consulate in El San Sabo. That won't keep us from being robbed, but it may keep us from getting killed. You need to hide our gold pouch back up there in the woods. Bury it if you can. You will have to dig with the machete since we left the shovel on the raft."

Jordanne did as instructed. Her trail into the bamboo thicket where she hid the treasure in a circle so she didn't double any sign she may have made on the way into and out of her hiding spot. She looped from the downstream side to the upstream side. When she returned, she was once again drenched in sweat, but triumphant. "They ain't gonna find our gold," she said. "Now what do I do? I know we need to boil water. We're almost out. Will a fire bring those sons of bitches right to us, though?"

"More than likely," he said. "I hate to be so damned helpless, but you are going to have to scout around and gather some firewood. We can screen the fire after we know the cartel boys have gone back upstream. You will have to figure out the food thing. The boat needs to be worked further up onto the gravel bar and the anchor tied on and planted to hold it. You'll want to unload the boat before you try to move it, but don't remove the engine. The gas tank needs to be refilled. There should be a filler neck in one of the gas cans. Sorry to lay all this on you, honey. If you'll bring me the binocs, I'll watch for the return of the cartel boats. I can see enough of the far bank of the river from here to see them go by."

She felt her heart lurch. Suddenly, she was the one in charge, including being his caretaker. Her love for him filled her with determination. She walked over to him, knelt beside him, and kissed him. She handed him the binoculars. "Don't worry," she said. "I can do this."

He alternately watched Jordanne's progress and the river. He marveled at the young woman's determined efforts. She worked tirelessly. During the first hour, she piled up an adequate supply of firewood. He advised her about starting the fire with a splash of fuel from one of the Jerry cans. "When we get ready to light the fire," he said, "I'll explain how to use some fuel to start it."

She stopped unloading the boat, stretched her back, and asked, "How do I set up a screen to hide the fire?"

"I have been studying that," he said. "If we start our fire before dark, it won't be as obvious as it would be in the dark. We can build it behind the boat. That should be screen enough. The trees will filter the smoke. After we boil water and fix dinner, we will need to scatter the fire. We can sleep under the tarp. You might want to cut something for bedding. Ferns seemed to be best on the raft. I saw some down toward the big river below where I fell."

"I'm glad I don't have to rig up a screen with the tarp. That was gonna be a bitch," she said. "The rest of this will be a snap." With that, she returned to her honey-do list and dug in.

It was midafternoon when he spotted the speedboats in their upriver return. He grinned to himself. Even though he and Jordanne were in dire straits, it amused him that they had eluded determined pursuit. It was only the temporary respite of the prey eluding the predator, but he couldn't help feeling a bit of smugness. "There they go!" he called to her. She was returning from the edge of the Rio El Diablo with her second armload of ferns. She turned and spied the gleaming white spumes zooming upriver and around a bend out of sight.

She grinned and shouted, "Go, you sons of bitches, go!" Alec laughed for the first time since he fell. She continued shaping up their camp. Moving the boat proved to be difficult, but she did so by seesawing the bow back and forth and pulling on the anchor rope, gaining enough to drag the stern out of the smaller river's current. "How much more do I need?" She panted.

Alec looked from his vantage point, checking the influence of the river on the stern. "Unless it rains and the river comes up, that should be good," he said. "Why don't we use some rope to extend the anchor line and tie the boat off to a tree? That way, we won't have to rely on just the anchor."

"Capital idea," she said. "Yeah, let's us do that." But she did it as she continued to slave away. The next item up was setting out the food stuff and preparation of a meal. The packet contained potatoes, flour, salt, loaves of bread, a large round block of cheese, peppers and plantains, beans, and rice. It was a generous stash for a trip with planned meal stops. For Alec and Jordanne who needed more of a fast-food menu, it was likely to be lacking.

Jordanne announced the food contents as she found them. When she was finished, she looked at Alec and said, "Don't ask 'What's for dinner?' I still have to build a fire and boil water."

"I hear you," he said. "Give me a slice of cheese, a crust of bread, and a plantain. I'll wait to wash it down with water. You are doing a fantastic job, babe. Fantastic job."

"Good. I'm not into cooking tonight. I'm about beat. So how about the fire?"

He instructed her to get a fire starter from the backpack. "Make sure it lights," he said. "Build up your wood stack over there behind the boat. Drag one of the Jerry cans over. What you're going to do is splash a small amount of gas onto the wood. You will want to then add some gas to the end of a stick. Pull your gas can well away from the fire. Stand back yourself, and using the fire starter, light the stick. Then toss it onto your fire. There will be a whoosh, so be sure you are moving back when you toss the firestick. Got it?"

"Can't you tell me as I go?"

"No. The gas evaporates quickly, so lighting has to be done smoothly and just as quick. I'll run through it again." After that instruction, she pulled off the task without a hitch. While she waited for the fire to burn down so that she could boil water, she flopped down beside Alec.

"I hope you like girls who stink," she said. "How are you feeling?"

"The pain is less. I expect my ass is swollen, so I'll have to live with that for a while. Then I'll be stiff and sore for a while. I don't think we can hit the river for a couple of days. We can wait until tomorrow to refill the fuel tank. When we do take off, you are probably going to have to push the boat into the water, start the engine, and maybe, even run the boat. Sorry."

"I was going to kiss you until you said all that. Now I've got to save my strength."

She boiled water until they both had enough to wash down their meals and fill their water bottles. Then she spread the fire out to burn down. "Now what?" she asked.

"Drag me to bed," he said.

"Roger," she said. "Can't I just throw the tarp over you?"

"If I could laugh, I would. I'd roll over there, but I want to see how much progress I've made."

With her help, he painfully managed to get to his feet and walk to the bed site. In trying to ease down, he fell on his right hip. The pain was a white-hot stab that caused him to scream. He twisted and squirmed while waiting for the pain to pass. She was unable to help him. Her anguish and fear, however, was printed upon her face, which drained her of color. When he was able to stabilize, resting on his left hip, he looked at her. "Hey!" he said cheerfully. "That wasn't so bad. Yeah, we're good now."

She began to cry as she knelt beside him. He put his arm around her and let her weep without saying anything. Finally, she looked at him. "What are we going to do?" she asked.

"Wait," he said. "Now that you have us all set up, that won't be so hard, will it?"

She looked around and took heart as she realized how much she had accomplished. "No. No, it won't be so hard."

"Now," he said, "we need to spread our net over us, tuck it under as well, and pull the tarp over the bed and our guns."

She slept like the dead. His was fitful and interrupted by pain. He spent hours doping out the next few days. He expected company. The question was, When and where? He hoped to be back on his feet within three days. He knew that running ahead of the pack was lost. Theirs would have to be a cat-and-mouse game that he hoped would not involve gunfire against the cartels.

The following day was spent with Jordanne finishing up what was left undone from the day before. She managed to fill the fuel tank from a Jerry can without too much spillage or too much advice from Alec. She used the twelve-by-fifteen-foot tarp to camouflage their boat. Using the binoculars, both kept watch on the big river, looking for fortune hunters as well as the cartel speedboats. They watched as the speedboats raced downriver. They were later coming back than the day before, which indicated they were searching further and further each day.

"They will probably start looking this way tomorrow," Alec observed. "God, I hope I'm back on my feet before they catch us in here. We need a story to tell them about the gold. What do you think of this? We donated the entire wad to the church because we didn't want to be hunted for it. That's how we got the boat. We will invite them to search the boat, the backpack, the woods around here, us. If they want our guns, fine. All we want is safe passage to El San Sabo."

"How much virtue do they have?"

"Well, none that I know of."

"So you are inviting them to search me?"

"Hadn't thought of that. Well, it's binding time then," he said.

"Oh, for Christ's sakes! That's not the way I like being felt up. I won't even let you do it with my tits flattened clear to my navel."

"Sorry, sweetheart," he said. "When they come to you, turn your pockets inside out. That might keep them from frisking you. You will have to have your hair up and your hat on. Pull the keeper thong up tight against your chin. You don't want them knocking your hat off. How well did you hide the gold pouch?"

She smiled. "Unless they have gold-sniffing dogs, they have no chance."

"Good. They will have someone with them who can speak English. Let me do the talking. If they speak to you, just shrug or use nonverbal communication. If you have to speak, keep it as short as you can. One word 'yes's and 'nos' would be best."

Alec spent a lot of time that day working his legs. Jordanne helped him flex his knees and stretch out his lower back. While painful, the exercise allowed him to get to his feet. With the aid of his walking stick, he was able to hobble about their campsite without her assistance. It made them both hopeful that they could renew their journey the next day. Their dinner that night included rice with sliced plantains and melted cheese. Jordanne topped it off with chopped pepper. They both thought it delicious. They turned in as darkness settled over the river. They lay in each other's arms, watching as the stars sweetened the velvet swash of the Milky Way. With hope in their hearts for a restart of their interrupted journey the next day, they both fell into a long peaceful night of sleep.

Jordanne woke with a yelp the next morning. Alec's response was to look at her sleepily, "What?"

"Oh god!" she whispered. "Who are these guys?"

He turned and rose to his elbows. Looking quickly around the small clearing of their camp, he saw natives armed with blowguns. "I don't know, but don't make any sudden moves. They don't look hostile, but they want something, that's for sure. Let's give it a minute and see what they want."

"What are those things they are pointing at us?"

"Blowguns."

"You mean those poison dart tubes?"

"Yes. Whatever they want, we have to do. Here comes their spokesman."

A small muscular man stepped out of a kind of dugout canoe and approached them. He was definitely one of the forest people featured in National Geographic films. He was scantily clad in skins and pierced through the nose and ears. He wasted no time with preliminaries and was sure of what he wanted. He pointed at Jordanne, waved for her to follow him, and strode back to his dugout, a two-person affair in which she was to become the second person. Frantically, she looked at Alec. "What should I do?"

"Go. If they were going to harm us, they already would have. But they still might, if we resist. They probably have a village somewhere upstream. Believe me, I'll follow in the boat. I'll make it happen. I won't be far behind. The boat is a lot faster than their dugouts."

In moments, the entire group of forest people disappeared, rapidly paddling their way upstream on the smaller river. Jordanne was a terrified prisoner, looking back as long as she could see the campsite. For hours, the paddlers kept a steady rhythm that seemed inexhaustible. With the passing time, she simply became numb. At first, she was certain that at any moment, she would be taken to shore, pulled from the dugout, and raped, pillaged, and burned. The natives showed no interest in her, however. There were no lascivious stares, no conversation that would lend fear of violation. They simply maintained a steady stroking of their paddles that sped their watercraft efficiently upstream.

As soon as the campsite was cleared of intruders, Alec began the process of stretching out his legs and back. Although painful, it was much less so than the day before. In an hour, he was moving reasonably well. Luckily, Jordanne had placed the refueled tank along with the two Jerry cans back into the boat. The empty can had been discarded at an edge of the clearing. The greatest task he feared, and he knew it, was moving the boat. He tackled that first when he felt he would be at his strongest. He couldn't do it. As much as he hated it, he finally resigned himself to having to stay another day and night in occurred to her that she needed to play the game. To the natives, this whole extravaganza was deadly serious. She couldn't think of anything else to do, so she knelt before the bed, spread her hands in a sweeping gesture from head to toe of the man, folded her hands, and began to pray. She trusted that her voice and the solemn way she spoke in English would seem "goddess like." Once started, she found much more to say than she thought she could possibly expound. Her prayers, however, were not only for the man, but also for her and Alec. She spent an hour and ceased when the man fell into an apparently deep and untroubled sleep. Then she spread her hands wide, encompassing the sleeping man before her, and looked at the medicine man. He nodded, rose, and signaled for her to follow him. He led her to the entrance of the hut.

There, the four men and their chair met her and bore her back to the former hut. An hour passed before they returned. Then they bore her to the main communal structure. For the rest of the evening, she was plied with food and drink. The food was good and bad. The drink was an unpleasant sour citrus-based and pulp-filled concoction that seemed somewhat fermented. It seemed to tickle the natives that she didn't enjoy it. She was afraid not to drink some of it, however, and did her best to politely imbibe a moderate amount. At last, the man who had striped her face called a halt to the festivities. He led her to a bedding platform that had been screened off for her. There, she found her clothes which she found had been laundered with the sweetly fragranced leaves. As surprising as that was, there was another. A sleeping gown of warm white cotton awaited her, folded upon the bed, which was adorned with a blanket and a pillow, both startlingly white. The entire platform was also enclosed by white mosquito netting. Jordanne was getting the idea that she was revered in some very special and serious way. She didn't take it lightly and slept well, feeling as though her soul had, in a strange way, been refreshed.

Alec was awake long before dawn and began planning his strategy for rescuing Jordanne. At first, he thought of going in guns blazing, hoping to frighten the whole horde back into the hills and giving him time to locate her, hustle her back to the boat, and beat it back downstream. As he thought about that, it occurred to him strange that he still had his guns. The more he thought, the more he felt that a saner approach would be to find the village and hope for a shore where he could beach the boat. He would have his weapons ready in case of a confrontation, but he would simply let events play out as they might. When daylight came, he went through the stretching regimen he had been using to get up and on his feet.

He was vastly relieved that the pain, while sharp at times, was much less. He was sure that the swelling had gone down substantially. Encouraged, he took his walking stick and began using it as a lever to move the boat toward the water. It took over an hour until he had the boat floating. Then he coiled up the rope that had tied off the boat to the tree. He stuffed the netting and tarp under the deck, tossed his walking stick into the boat, along with the backpack, and finally dropped the anchor and its rope coiled around it into the boat. He bellied his way into the boat over the starboard gunwale. The pain was gathering in his tailbone and lower back, but he gritted his teeth and dropped the engine off its dock-rest step. When he had the fuel line attached and primed to the engine, he faced the most difficult task. Pulling the starting cord. Fortunately, the engine sprang to life on the second pull. Again, he gave thanks to the priest for the quality of the entire set up. Then he was off on the trail of Jordanne and the forest people.

Jordanne rose the next morning to find that her white gown and slippers had been removed. So she's dressed in her regular clothes. The natives made sure she was offered food left over from the night before. She ate sparingly and spent the next couple of hours close to the beach at the river's edge. The people were going about their daily lives, not really paying much attention to her, but clearly holding her in a reverent and exalted position. Her patient was also up and around, clearly back in charge and loved by his people. She watched anxiously downriver. At length, she heard the unmistakable sound of an engine. The sound grew louder. She rose and walked to the water's edge and waited for the boat to come into view. She experienced an overwhelming sense of relief when she recognized the boat. She waved gaily, and when the boat nosed into the beach, she grabbed the anchor and walked it up the bank. She attached its rope to the bow eye, tied it off, and tightened the anchor. "So how are you?" she asked.

"Not as good as you," he said, clearly mystified by the scene before him. He was largely ignored. There were no threatening figures with blowguns. "What gives?" he asked.

"I am a goddess," she said.

"A what?"

"Goddess."

"Okay," he said. "So how do I behave?"

"Take it seriously. They do. Don't ask why because I don't know. Only three of them have spoken in English. Two of them spoke one word. The other, two. They have treated me like something supernatural ever since I got here. One of the words was 'goddess,' and that's how they treated me. Can you get out of the boat?"

"I don't know. I can't kick the motor up. I'll slide over and help if you can give me a hand."

She moved in behind the boat, wading in her boots. As she started to lift the motor, she was suddenly assisted by a pair of the native men, who didn't know exactly what was needed, but who easily lifted the motor until it clicked into the rest stop. Alec signaled them to stop, and they dropped it neatly onto the rest. "Wow, they really are quick to help, aren't they?" he said.

"Let's see if we can get you out of there," she said. He scooted back over to the gunwale and tried lifting a leg over the edge. She leaned into the boat, trying to lift under his arm. She had no sooner begun when more of the native men came to their aid. They could see that Alec was unable to help himself to any extent, so they grabbed him and lifted him out. That the lift was terribly painful for him was plain for Jordanne to see. She moved in swiftly to keep him from falling. The men stood uneasily, not knowing what else to do until Jordanne pointed to Alec and then to the hut where she had prayed over their headman. The men understood and seized Alec in a four-man carry, which was the most excruciating pain he had felt yet. With great effort, however, he kept from crying out.

The trip was swift, and soon, they had him laid out on the bed previously occupied by the chief. Then they left, and the medicine man took their place. He looked at Alec and shrugged quizzically. Jordanne leaned over, unbuttoned Alec's pants, helped him roll over onto his left hip, and pulled his pants down to expose a large purple bruise extending from his tailbone across his hip and up into his lower back. Despite himself, he groaned audibly.

The medicine man sprang into action. He looked carefully at the bruise, probing it with his fingers. Then he leaned down and carefully smelled the entire ugly mess. Finally, he began building a poultice from a host of materials that neither Alec, nor Jordanne, cared to know anything about. When the poultice was ready, the man spread it liberally over the bruise, working it in with brisk kneading. Alec was at the point of howling unabashedly when the ministration ended. The poultice was thickly caked over the entirety, including deeply into the crack of Alec's ass. While there was considerable heat involved, it was not unbearable. The medicine man patted a cover of cloth-like material over his treatment. Then he left.

"My god! I thought he was gonna kill me," Alec said.

"How does it feel, though?" she asked.

"Well, pretty good," he said. "Whatever he has in that stuff is making the pain go away. I think it's numbing everything, and look, I can move my legs without pain. Let me see if I can roll over." While somewhat painful, he did so without assistance. He was surprised that he could lie on his back pain free. "I can't believe this," he said, relief clearly limning his face. "Let's stay a week!"

She laughed and kissed him. "Let's not press our luck. Maybe a couple of days, if you get well enough for us to leave. Or not. Wait until you see how they feed and what they drink. You'll probably want to leave tomorrow."

"I was wondering, by the way, about your makeup. Is that part of the princess mystique?"

"It's goddess. Don't try to demote me already. And yes. My makeup man applied it before I attended my patient."

"You had a makeup artist?"

"Yes, I did. He looked deep into my eyes and said, 'Goddess.'"

"Well! I am a lucky man, being in love with a real down-to-earth goddess. Yes, indeed. One lucky son of a bitch."

"Just don't let it go to your head. Don't forget it either."

After an evening in which both of them were treated like royalty, Alec agreed. One night on the town was enough. That he would be eternally grateful for the poultice that put him back on his feet nearly pain free, notwithstanding, he was determined to leave the next day. There was one problem, however. The river had come up after a heavy evening rain, and the next morning the boat was gone. With gesticulations from Jordanne, a rescue team was launched. Alec and Jordanne were carried along in two-person crafts of the type that was used to kidnap her. The boat was found after an hour, tangled up in brush at the edge of the river. Water had lapped over the upstream gunwale. Despite his best effort, Alec was unable to start the motor. "What do we do?" Jordanne asked.

"Can you get these guys to help if I show them how to row?"

"Maybe." She began with more gesticulation. Her prestige held. The natives used their hands to empty most of the water out of the boat. Alec affixed the oars and demonstrated how to row. The men quickly caught on and, two of them, one on each oar, began a coordinated effort that moved the boat against the current. It was slow but steady. The men traded off. Those who were rowing had their own one-man dugouts pressed to the sides of the two-man dugouts that were used for Alec and Jordanne. To affect that, one man rode in each of the two-man crafts holding a dugout on each side, his own and one belonging to one of rowers. It took four hours to return to the village. The motorboat was hauled well up on the beach, and the anchor supplemented by rope tied to a tree. Alec popped the cover off the motor. Everything was soaked. While he didn't know for sure, he was hopeful that simply letting the motor dry out might rectify the problem. Whatever, it was clear they would by staying at least another night.

Their sleeping quarters were again in the ersatz hospital. The medicine man came and gave Alec another thorough working over. It was much less painful and thoroughly restorative. Alec was able to walk easily on his own to the community center where they were again regaled and fed the native food washed down with the natives' favorite drink. Alec leaned over to Jordanne at one point and whispered, "Don't bother to get the recipe for this old mule's piss. I can't stand it. I'm drinking it to be polite."

"Really!" she said. "Well, what if I told you I already have it?"

"What are you trying to do? Get a divorce before we are even married?"

"Is that your way of proposing?"

"Not what I had in mind, but would you?"

Just then, another meat dish was pressed upon them. That he had inadvertently, and in a left-handed way, popped the question hung over their heads for the rest of the meal and evening. When they finally returned to their hospital room, both filled to bursting, he followed up with, "Well?"

"Well, what?"

"You know 'Well what'?" he insisted.

"Do you remember what you said one time about my pickup lines? Let me see if I remember. Oh yeah, I remember now. You said, 'You smooth-talking bitch.' Does that ring a bell?"

"Oh, come on, sweetheart. That was too long ago and too much blood under the bridge! You can't be serious about that."

"You're right. I'm not, but the man I marry will make a proper proposal on his knee, with a ring in his hand. Period, end of report."

"You are saying I still have a chance then."

"I'll think about it. Now, let's go to bed."

The next morning, after sharing another meal with the forest people, Alec and Jordanne, with the help of the natives, positioned the boat in the river with the motor down. Alec pumped the primer bulb tight, pulled out the choke, and set the throttle to Start. Jordanne held her breath. With no thought of his back pain, Alec gave the starter cord a strong pull, then another, and another. Finally, on the seventh pull, the motor belched, turned over, and started. It was running roughly, however, and Alec figured out what may have happened. He hit the kill switch. "What's the matter?" she asked.

"I think water got into the gas tank," he said. "We're going to have to dump it and refill it with gas from one of the Jerry cans."

"No way to save it?"

"Afraid not. Damn, that means we are down to half the fuel we started with. Somehow, we are going to need to refuel, or we'll be doomed to rowing and floating on the current."

Alec dumped the fouled fuel and added the contents of one of the Jerry cans to the fuel tank. He made a gift of the empty can to the village chief. It was like Santa Claus had made a surprise visit. Alec felt very pleased with himself and humble at the same time. Jordanne was proud of him and smiled her pleasure. Once again, he attempted to start the motor. It caught on the third pull but still ran rough. He killed it and began looking around at the engine. He spied a gas-filled bulb filter, popped off the retainer ring, and dumped the fuel out on the ground. He replaced the glass bowl and pumped the primer bulb, refilling the glass with fuel. Once again, he pulled vigorously on the starter cord. It took a half dozen pulls, but the motor started, sputtered for a bit, but finally leveled off, running smoothly. "All right!" he yelled triumphantly. "Let's say goodbye and get the hell outta here!"

They turned to the people who had all gathered to watch the process of starting the motor. Alec took off his hat and bowed formally and courteously to the headman. Jordanne smiled and waved. He retrieved the anchor and placed it in the bow of the boat. They both stepped in, and he reversed the engine, pulling them out into center of the river, where he kicked it into forward and turned the boat in a sharp vee and hit the throttle. They roared away, leaving their friends staring at their departure.

It was a quick trip back to their old camp. Alec throttled down to idle and pulled up on the gravel of the beach. He killed and pulled the motor up to the dock-rest stop to clear the prop. Jordanne, taking her cue as first mate, tossed the anchor out, followed it, and set it in the sand above the gravel. The boat swung its stern around in the current and held. Alec stepped out at the bow and looked around. Jordanne stretched out her back, bending over and placing her hands flat on the ground. Then she straightened up and looked at him, "How's the back?" she asked.

He shrugged his shoulders and bent over with his hands reaching his knees "What back?" he said. "That guy could make millions with that poultice. It was a wonder cure. I've never seen the like."

"It is amazing," she said. "I prayed for you too."

"You did?"

"Yeah, I prayed for you and the chief. You both got well. Spooky, isn't it?"

"Woo! That's beyond my pay grade, my dear. What isn't is this camp."

"What's different about it?"

"The Jerry can's gone. The bed's been kicked apart, and it looks like an invasion took place back in there in the bamboo. I think someone came in here and started looking for our gold. If you think you can still find it, let's go see if it's still there."

He carried the machete and followed her into the thicket on the same loop she had made in hiding the pouch. She slipped easily through the bamboo, with him bulling along behind her. She finally stopped at a tiny clearing in the near solid stand of vegetation. "There," she said and stepped into a small opening in the wall. He looked and could see nothing indicating the location of something buried. "Dig," she commanded.

"Okay, boss," he said and began rooting in the ground with the machete. After a few minutes, he felt the machete hit a resistance. A little later, their gold was back in their possession. Once more she slipped along, and he bulled his way, cursing behind her on her path back to the river and their old camp.

When he had stowed the gold pouch in the backpack, she asked, "What's the plan?"

He said, "We have to think this thing out. We're short on fuel, and we've lost our head start. We'll stay here till it gets dark, then we'll go, real slow, all night. If we can get in ten hours at ten miles an hour, that's a hundred miles. We'll hole up and rest during the day. It's going to take us three nights and three days to get to the mouth of the river. The rest of today, we need to prepare food, one meal a day, plus a couple more, to carry us through. I've got to see if I can get the guns cleaned up. The pistols and ammo are in the backpack, the rifle is pushed way up in the bow, but I'm sure all of them got wet. This thing with the cartels is going to be a cat-and-mouse game, sweetheart. If you have any of those prayers of yours left, now's the time to use 'em."

As the day wore on, the two of them prepared for what lay ahead. He built a fire, and she did the cooking while he cleaned the guns. At times, they were able to take breaks together. They talked and mused about what had happened and what they hoped for when they escaped the country. It was during one of these that Alec broached the reason for her kidnapping. "I was wondering something," he said. "What did the village chief do when he first saw you?"

"Well, he perked right up. Seemed relieved and, I don't know, hopeful. Almost spiritual. Why?"

"Voodoo," he said.

"Oh, bullshit!" she exclaimed. "What on Earth made you say that?"

"I was working south of here one time, and the natives there believed in a hybrid form of it. They believed in the needles through stuff that belonged to the one being hexed or cursed. When the subject being targeted found out about it, he would become sick, lie down, and refuse food and drink until a hex breaker could be summoned to do incantations with smoke and the waving of certain bird feathers over the body of the afflicted. Stuff like that. The hex breaker had to be a young woman known to have the power. But if a chieftain were hexed, it took a white goddess to break the hex, but not just any white woman. They meant a blonde with white hair, dressed in stunningly beautiful head-to-toe white, not even a fleck of dirt on her shoes. Sort of like the virginate bride. If the hex breaker didn't show up within about four days, the poor sap kicked the bucket from lack of water. Look at your hair, sweetheart. I hate to say it, but they bleached it out. Looks great, but it is much lighter than it was."

She pulled her hair from around her right shoulder. "Yeah, you're right. Is it white clear to the roots?"

"All the way. Marilyn Monroe would be envious of your hair right now."

"Why don't they call on an old woman, then? Their hair is always white from the roots out."

"Old people don't have the power to lift the hex."

"Okay, so where did I get this power?"

"You didn't, but they didn't know that. But since you were praying in English, they were convinced you had it. They couldn't understand anything you said. You were convincing that way. If you had been praying in Spanish, it might have been different because a good number of them probably understand Spanish."

"So you are saying I'm not a goddess?"

"Well, as the old saying goes: 'You were queen for a day.' Now you can wash your face."

As night began coming on and they were preparing to launch the boat and hit the big river, he queried another question to her. "Did you ever wonder why there have been times when we heard monkeys and times when we didn't?"

"No, I didn't pay attention, I guess. Why would that be?"

"Well, a little bit of a story first. Sometime back, I was working on a job on an island in the South Pacific that should have been alive with monkeys. Surrounding islands were. But I was there for a week and never saw, nor heard, a single one. I was working with an island native toward the end of the week, so I asked him about it. He said, 'Ah, the monkey. We eat him.'"

Jordanne looked at him for a moment then, in a horrified voice, said, "You're saying that maybe the natives here eat monkeys?"

"No, maybe about it. Those who have blowguns, especially. Rifles scare the monkeys away. If you remember, after every time we shot the rifle, it got really monkey quiet for a long time. That doesn't happen with a blowgun. The monkey troop takes off, but in a day or so, it can be hunted again."

"Oh my god! Are you saying we ate monkey back up there in the village?"

"Yes, I am."

"How do you know for sure?"

"I found a fingernail. They just didn't serve you that particular portion, but if they had, they would have thought nothing of it.

I didn't say anything because I didn't want to freak you out. That would have been unseemly for a goddess," he said, grinning ghoulishly at her.

"Jesus Christ, what else is this country gonna throw at me? I feel like puking my guts out right now!"

"Bucket list," he said, grinning again.

"Some bucket list. I suppose if you rescue me from a cartel whorehouse, you'll say I can cross that off my bucket list too," she said bitterly.

"Naw, I would just leave you there and let you enjoy being their goddess."

"Oh, for Christ's sake, why don't you just give us up to the cartels and you can sign on to be my pimp!"

"Hell, I'd never be able to afford you if I did that!"

Darkness had cloaked the river, so Alec explained to her their procedure. "We are going to run the center of the river," he said, "but at night, the river gets eerie. Crocs and caiman hunt and move around in the dark, but they give off bright eyeshine when they're hit by a light. They also hang pretty close to shore. If we run into any out in the middle, they'll be those big bulls crossing the river. We don't want to hit them. You are going to be up front with the flashlights. Keep a sharp lookout. After you get your night vision, you will be able to spot them as slow as we are going to be moving. If you see anything like a dark shadow, hit it with your light. Their eyes will pop right out. Then yell 'left or right' to let me know which way to steer. If you yell, 'left,' I will steer that way. "Right," I'll go that way. Don't worry about false alarms. The more, the merrier! False alarms won't hurt us, but capsizing this boat from hitting one of those big bastards will be different altogether."

He steered out into the gentle current and turned to the east, moving at a modest pace to conserve fuel. He knew that bends in the river at night could be tricky. The river would wall off at even a fairly modest bend. The problem would then be to figure out which way it bent. Patience with himself and with Jordanne, especially, was going to be paramount.

Their progress was methodical. At first, she yelled seemingly all the time, but as she got better, their swerving back and forth became less and less. A few times, she saved them from collisions with brush and logs. Each time he called over the sound of the engine, "Good girl!" or "Well done!" Twice in the first few hours the river took bends, they had to probe to find direction. Once they found themselves too close to shore, and Jordanne had to yell, "Stop! Back up!" to keep them from running aground. As the boat swung around after they had emergency reversed enough to make the turn, she directed her light's beam down and toward the shore they had averted. The shoreline and the water around them were filled with eyeshine, some of it moving rapidly toward them. That unnerved both of them. Jordanne shrank back from the side of the boat and dropped down on the seat as Alec gunned the engine. He spun the boat, and it quickly came up on plane, but not before the skid plate hit one of the beasts and bounced the engine up out of the water. It raced insanely for a moment before dropping down and shooting the boat back into deeper and safer water. Alec dropped the motor into neutral and let the boat drift on its own. "Are you all right?" he called to her.

"No! How could anybody be all right? Are you all right? Don't tell me that didn't get to you! What would have happened if we had run aground right there?"

"Oh shit! I don't want to think about it. No one would ever find out, that's for sure. You ready to get going?"

"Oh yeah! Lead on, Mr. Cousteau. I'm getting so used to near-death experiences that I can't wait for the next one."

"I think he was more an ocean-going man. We are more like Bear Grylls."

"Wonderful! Maybe we can get a TV series too."

Their probing finally yielded the hidden turn, and they were able to motor the center of the river for several more hours. Jordanne grew weary of standing up all the time and began alternating between sitting and standing spells. Sleep kept knocking at their doors. Alec was also letting down his guard, his alertness diminished to the hum of the engine. He checked the shorelines to make sure that they were pretty well centered in the push of the current. It was when Jordanne was standing that she didn't see the huge shadow that bulked up out of the water just before they hit it. The boat reared up and pitched wildly to port. Alec was slung to starboard, losing contact with the control arm of the motor. Jordanne was pitched to starboard, over the side, and into the water. The great crocodile, as surprised as they were, lashed out his massive tail, turning the boat sideways, just missing her, and thrusting himself away from the danger it thought the boat represented.

Jordanne surfaced, screaming, "Alec, help me! Help me!" Over and over, her terrified screams rent the night. He clambered back and cut the engine and dove forward to where he could see her struggling toward the boat. The tail thrust of the croc had arrested the motion of the boat, but it was still drifting slowly away from her. He looked frantically around her, trying to spot the behemoth. From the tail slash that had whipped and struck the boat, he knew that the size of the croc was in the fifteen-foot range, and that it would weigh well over a thousand pounds. He was also aware that it would turn and surge back to see what it had struck, seeking prey. That it feared nothing also flashed through his mind. He was petrified at the thought of seeing Jordanne seized in its massive jaws and pulled under and away. "Jordanne!" he screamed. "Swim! Swim! Don't tread water!" In the filtered light sheen of the river, he could see the turn of the crocodile. Her thrashing gave it a perfect beacon. It was forty to fifty feet away, she was fifteen. Somehow, Alec's screams caused her to swim. In her panicked, adrenaline riddled state, and she moved with amazing swiftness, given how she was dressed. Her baggy pants gave him a handle that he seized, and as she grabbed the side of the boat, his strength aided by fear swept her up and over with her body barely touching the gunwale as they bowled over together back into the boat. She landed on top of him just as the massive collision of the croc thrust the boat sideways, dumping them back toward the open maw of the great beast, its head jacked up on the side of the boat. The only thing that saved them was that the croc had launched too late to get enough of his body above the gunwale to spill them back into the water. It snapped its jaws at them a couple of times before its massive weight pulled it back into the water.

Alec immediately scrambled to the stern of the boat. "Jordanne!" he bellowed. "Get down, don't stand up!" He set the throttle handle to start, jerked the starter cord, and felt a massive wave of relief wash over him as the engine burst to life. He immediately hit max go. The boat jerked spasmodically before he aligned the bow and the engine, but it quickly leveled out and bore them to safety.

He kept them at top speed for a while but finally twisted the throttle handle to Stop and let the boat glide to a halt, keeping the bow pointed downriver. "Do you want to talk about it?" he asked.

"No. It doesn't do any good to talk about all the things that keep happening to us. There is also no good in you holding me so I can cry like the maiden in distress. It's time for me to man up, spit in the water, and say, 'Let's get on with it, Jones.' You have made the point over and over that this trip is fifty-fifty, life or death. So let's do that and hope we win the lottery. Let me change clothes first." Without saying a word, he waited until she stripped, redressed, and signaled she was ready. He reset the throttle. She resumed her spot in the bow, and they motored on into the night.

Morning began as a smudge of gray in the east. It also brought with it the promise of rain. Alec began looking for a spot to pull in. The further they got toward the coast, the flatter the country became, and the thicker the jungle growth became as if it seemed to try to take over the land and the river slicing through it. Finding a place to beach the boat proved to be tricky. The river shallowed out toward the bank, and mudbanks that threatened to ground the boat were everywhere. It was nearly full light with a light rain falling when he spotted a small stream that poured into the river. He pitched the motor up into half rest and had Jordanne come sit with him in the stern to help keep the prop under water. They proceeded under slow idle, barely making headway against the stream flowing out of the dense foliage of the jungle. "How far up are we going to go?" she asked.

"Just enough to get out of sight of the river," he said.

"I'm not seeing anywhere to pull into the bank," she said.

"I don't either. Let's anchor in the water, grab a bite to eat, and see if we can get some sleep. If this rain is just a steady drizzle, we are going to use it as cover and head out. We won't travel as long, but I would like to do that and stay off the river tonight. What do you say?"

"I like it. We should be able to move somewhat faster and not have to waste fuel motoring around in the dark, trying to figure out where the river went. I suppose we'll use a little more fuel, but at least we'll be able to see where we are going. I'm also getting damned sick and tired of things that go bump in the night. Let me know when to toss the anchor."

After their adrenaline-soaked night, the two choked down a handful of their precooked rice, which she had spiced with salt. They each drank a half bottle of water. Then they lay down on adjacent bench seats, covered themselves with netting and their tarp. For four hours, they died. The metal of their beds woke them. It was still raining, a steady soaker that was unaccompanied by wind. The surface of the river was flat and shrouded by a cloying fog. "We finally got a break," Alec said. They retrieved the anchor, turned the boat, and eased out on the big water. The fog was excellent cover. They stowed their netting in the backpack. They sat together under the tarp and motored solemnly along. Jordanne held the folded tarp to catch runoff into their water bottles. Both drank as much water as they could, and then they stowed their filled bottles in the backpack.

At midafternoon, they began looking for a place to duck in for the night. Alec felt they had made good progress during their five or six hours on the water. "How far did we go today?" she quizzed him.

"About a hundred miles. But we're probably going to use the rest of our fuel starting tomorrow. I figure we have in the neighborhood of a hundred fifty miles to go, at most. I have no idea what it'll be like running against the tide. I fear running out of fuel."

"Aren't there marinas down there somewhere to get more."

"Yes. Cartel-controlled marinas. Pulling into one of those would be like pulling into their private ones and announcing, 'Here we are. We'd like a fill-up! Don't bother asking about gold. It's ours. And no. You can't have it. You can't have the other gold from the Rio Estrella, either. That's her, and she doesn't work in whorehouses.' That ought to work, don't you think?"

"Funny. Ha ha! So what happens when we do run out?"

"We float and row."

"For how far?"

"Hopefully less than fifty miles. This river is running a slow current, and the priest said it has a braided mouth. That last fifty could take three or four days. What could go wrong?"

She looked at him and frowned. "This is getting a little late in the game to be flip or sarcastic. We still have to run the gauntlet of the cartels. What's that going to be like?"

"How do you want it, straight or with 'maybe, but if, if only, or on the other hand' kind of stuff?"

"Try straight first."

"Here's what I know. There are four big cartels in this country, but a gob of smaller wannabes. The big guys would knock us off if we were handy. They won't waste a lot of time and manpower on us though. They certainly wouldn't fight each other for us. It's the other cats we have to watch out for. To them, we are big fish. They will also fight each other to get us. They are territorial and work like hell to grab off a piece of the other cat's territory and business. They are all into drugs, primarily, although they do have other business interests."

"Let me guess. Whorehouses."

"Yeah. Cheap ones, where I can afford you."

"Jesus, if I ever get out of this shithole country, I'll never come back. Whose boats were those we were watching?"

"Probably North Coast or Medellin. Two of the big boys. The ones that found our camp on Voodoo River, I'm thinking, were of the other ilk."

"Well, which ilk are we going to have to dodge from here. Aren't we about past the turnaround point of those boats that had us scared shitless?"

"We're close. But then, there are the boats that come up from the coast. The smaller outfits sort of crisscross the river. We got 'em coming and going. Sort of like Earth crossing meteors. We just have to hope we don't get hit before we get to El San Sabo and the consulate. Then the real shit hits the fan!"

"What do you mean by that?"

"Well, think about this. Our gold is not really our gold. Colombia has very strict regs regarding removing minerals from their country. They will want in the neighborhood of 90 percent. We, on the other hand, want to leave here with 90 percent. That gives us about forty grand worth of clout to find someone to fly us out to where we can connect with flights to the US. Once there, we still have to figure out how to get the gold past customs and the IRS if we want to cheat. At best, I figure, if we play it straight with American customs, our take is going to be about a quarter million after US taxes. I have no qualms about hustling our gold past Colombian authorities. They've sold out to the cartels anyway."

"Jesus! Is the 'on the other hand' version as bleak as that?"

"It's about the same. Sorry, but the fun has just begun."

"Why don't you just throw the gold into the river and let's be done with it and continue our trip like every other fool American tourist?"

"You. You, as I keep trying to tell you, are as good as our gold, except that you are the gold that keeps on giving and giving and giving. If we can get you out of here, we deserve to get the gold out too after all we've been through. Somehow, sweetheart, we're getting out of here. You, me, and the gold."

They continued searching for a place to stop and spend the night. At a sharp snake's bend in the river, where it narrowed to flow between two great limestone ridges that were jungle ridden, and that pinched the river into a somewhat narrow gorge, they were able to find a small beach they could run the boat up far enough to keep it stabilized with the anchor set out on shore. They also heaved it up as far as they could, then set about preparing a bed for the night.

The rain had stopped, but the jungle dripped. Alec told Jordanne not to help with gathering bedding material, but to set out something for them to eat. It would be cold. There would be no fire. He took the machete and began hacking off boughs to make them a bed. It would be on the ground. He didn't have enough daylight to make a platform. By wrapping up in netting and laying the tarp over the boughs so they could fold it back over them and by tucking it in, he figured they would be protected from the drip of the trees and from the bugs that invariably came out at night. So far, the netting and tarp were proving to be another form of gold. When he finished his chore, he was soaking wet from sweat within and rain drip without. He tossed his last load of boughs on the bed pile and smiled at Jordanne, who was standing ready with the netting and tarp. "See why I didn't want you helping. I'm going to change into my other clothes. Tomorrow should be warm and sunny, so we'll stay here long enough to dry out our wets. What's for dinner!"

She tossed the netting onto the bed and spread the tarp out far enough for them to sit. "As soon as you are changed, I will serve you."

He stripped and changed in the dark. The sun had gone down, and as happens in dark places, there was no afterglow. Darkness had dropped on the land like a rock. He stuffed his wet clothes into the backpack on top of Jordanne's. When he turned to see about their meal, she was sitting on the tarp. "Come sit," she said, "and give me your clasp knife."

"Are we being formal?"

"Oh, yeah. Right here in Pig Turd Alley."

He unfolded the knife and handed it to her, handle first. Then he sat cross-legged beside her. She took a boiled potato and sliced off a chunk, salted it, and told him to open his mouth. She found his lips with a kiss, and they played tongue tag for a moment. Then she stuffed the potato into his maw. He chewed it thoroughly, swallowed, and said, "Delicious! I think I'll have another." She repeated the process as she fed him potato and a small rice ball. She ate the same amount of food as he.

"And sir, how did you enjoy your meal?" she asked.

"It was lovely. I have never been served like that before. However, do you have ulterior motives?"

"Why, yes, I do. I'm practicing getting ready to work in a whorehouse. You're my very first customer!"

"I am truly honored," he responded. "What, pray tell, does a lady of the evening do next?"

"She lays out a tarp on the boughs and screws like a mink."

"Then," he said, "let me assist you with that tarp!"

Chapter 10

The following morning dawned bright and clear as Alec had thought it would. When the sun reached their beach, they spread out the wet clothes on the deck of the boat. Then they lolled about doing nothing. It was pleasant as they turned the clothing and talked about the problem of finding a plane and flying out of country. "Do you think we can bribe another priest?" She wanted to know.

"Maybe. We don't have an introduction to set us up this time. I'm wondering if we can somehow hide our gold in luggage and petition the consulate for help in flying out legitimately."

"How would you do that?"

"Don't worry about that. I'll show you what I have in mind when we get settled into our hotel room in El San Sabo."

As they were chatting, the sound of a speedboat came pounding up the river. At first, it was muffled by the dense noise buffer of the jungle, but it burst around the bend of the river, like sudden thunder. Alec leaped and shoved Jordanne into the covering trees, where he had cut their bedding boughs.

Out of sight, they watched as an I/O model speedboat came racing by. It looked brand-new. Yellow banded on white, with an open hull shaped with matching speed slots, it was a surprise to the spectators back in the trees. Even more surprising were the passengers. Besides the driver, there were two other men, one on either side of the motor box cover, crouched in the shelter of the transom. Each was armed with a submachine gun, aimed back down the river. The boat swept through the S curve of the river at its maximum speed. It looked like it was moving at a hundred miles an hour but was probably doing something like eighty. Even so, it was breathtaking. The occupants did not see the pair staring at them as they sped by. Alec was stepping out of the trees when another rumble preceded a second boat. He quickly returned to his hiding place and pulled Jordanne down with him to kneel while the second boat shot by. It, too, was new. It sported a bright-red deck above a white hull, with speed slots along the sides. It was also moving at a high rate of nervous tension. The men in it were the driver and two gunners, all looking forward and crouched down behind low wind screens. So intent was their focus upon what lay beyond the curve of the river upstream that they also failed to note the small boat hauled out on the side of the river.

"What is that all about!" she asked.

"Gang warfare, I'm guessing," he said. "Some dispute between the little guys I told you about. The crisscrossers. Something has them pissed off, and they plan to settle it man to man. Let's listen for gunfire."

"You said those boats were from the cartels, now you are saying they are from the wannabes. Which is it?"

"Well, even the wannabes have good equipment. They deal in millions. The big four deal in billions. I doubt the big boys would fight pitched battles with one boat apiece. That's why I think this is a local dispute of small dimension for this country."

It wasn't long before they were rewarded. A battle between the two boats was taking place around the bend upstream of their beach. They could only guess how it played out. It lasted for most of half an hour. There were bursts of gunfire that lasted on a sustained basis, followed by brief rattles of fire, a bit of silence, the roaring of boats running in circles, more gunfire, some sustained, some sporadic, and then a great silence punctuated by no sounds of the battle, not even the gunning of the boat motors.

"It's over," Alec said.

"Who do you think won? Red or yellow."

"I don't think either one won. I think they slaughtered everyone on both boats. Let's wait. The boats will come floating around the bend in an hour or so."

"Why won't they sink?"

"That flotation stuff again. They will list and take on water until they sink to the hull line, but that's all. A boat like that got beached on a big rock in the Grand Canyon one time. They shot it full of holes with military fifty caliber from a helicopter. Wouldn't sink. They finally burned it."

The time seemed to creep. It was close to an hour and a half when the first boat, the red one, came drifting around the corner, listing heavily on its port side. "Okay," Alec said, "let's check her out."

They had already shifted their boat off its resting place, so it floated easily stern downstream. Jordanne set their anchor and line into the boat, pushed the stern into deeper water, and jumped into the boat at the bow. Alec fired up the motor, and they shot across the river to examine the wreckage. What they found confirmed their suspicions. All three men were dead. All from multiple gunshot wounds. Drying blood was smeared everywhere, bleak testimony to the men's determination to keep firing at their enemy as they scrambled about the boat even in their death throes. Alec prowled the boat. Jordanne stayed in the twelve-footer, keeping it positioned against the crippled speedboat. All he could find of any value was the submachine guns and a bag of unused clips of ammunition. He handed both guns and the bag to her before stepping out of the speedboat and into their boat. "Let's go see the other one," he said.

"What are we gonna do with those guys?"

"Those guys? We're going to let those guys float on down the river. We are going to have one hell of a time getting through a drug-fueled gang war, my dear. We don't have time to play nice with its casualties."

The yellow boat was in worse shape than the red one. It was sinking stern down at such an angle that all but one of the combatants had fallen into the water. That one was draped over the transom. At any moment, he was set to slide into the abyss. Alec slowly glided around the corpse of the boat. "Can you see anything in there we can use?" he asked her.

"Another gun and a bag."

"See if you can grab 'em."

Jordanne leaned over, gained a grip on the speedboat, and pulled the two boats together. Then she reached into the yellow boat and pulled the submachine gun into their boat. That was shortly followed by the ammo bag.

"Is there anything else in there that we can use?" he asked her.

"No."

"Then we're outta here."

"What about that guy?"

"Same deal. His friends will take care of him unless he slides into the water, then the crocs or caiman will. We need to go break camp and get away from this mess. Someone is bound to come looking for their boats and their friends."

Upon their return to the beach, they looked at their armaments haul. All three guns were nine-millimeter AR types converted to fully automatic. Only one contained an empty clip. The other two contained a full clip and a clip two-thirds full. The bags contained ten additional full thirty round banana clips. "Do you know how to shoot these things?" he asked.

"Not a clue."

"Well, no time like the present."

She looked alarmed. "Won't that give us away?"

"After the fusillade, probably not. It will sound like cleanup. These guns make us formidable. Just having them and holding them in plain sight elevates us from prey to predator. Being able to shoot them moves us up another notch. We need to do this."

"Jesus Christ! Yes, Mr. and Mrs. America come to Colombia. You'll love having to shoot your way back out! And don't you, Mr. Jones, be telling me to cross this off a goddamned bucket list either!"

"Woo, testy, testy! Remind me not to get in front of anything you plan to shoot from here on out."

"Yeah, I'll remind you all right. So what do I do?"

"Okay. You know how loud shooting gets, so don't let that affect what you are doing. Makes you flinch and miss. There are three things you need to know about. First is inserting the clips. You rip out the empties and slam in the fulls. Let's practice on this one with the empty clip."

Gold of the Rio Estrella

For the next couple of minutes, they each did the rip and slam several times. She was able to do both adequately after five or six attempts.

"Now, let's look at these two," he said, handing her the one with the full clip. "These things don't have safeties. That happens when you take your finger off the trigger. Other than that, when the firing hammer is forward, you can't fire it by pulling on the trigger. You must jerk it back to set it. Then you are hot. Let's give it a try. No finger on the trigger! Keep that damned barrel always pointed up unless you are going to shoot. Got it?"

"Got it. So I pull on this thing."

"Hold it! Watch me. Jesus, you could have stitched up the boat. Don't be in a great big hurry. Set the butt on your hip. Hold the gun in your left hand, with the barrel pointed up. With your right, jerk the lever back in one move to where it sets. One move, Jordanne! If you don't, you will jam the gun."

He showed her how to do it. When he had his cocked, he added another admonition. "Now, this thing is like a mouse trap set to spring. It's just as touchy too. Okay, see that grip sticking out below the barrel? You will, firmly with your left hand, hold the gun into your hip. The gun will try to climb as it fires, so you always hold low to start and control that upward movement through the target. As soon as you've gone high, rip back down. Keep shooting until you've emptied the clip, or your target is gone. When you let off the trigger, the gun stops firing. To start again, rip the slide back and pull the trigger. Watch me, then we'll have you try it. I'm going to shoot into the water so you can watch how the pattern walks up."

He triggered a line across the water, and when it terminated, he pulled the gun back down and traced the pattern down to where it started. "See what I did?"

"Sort of," she said. "You went up and brought it back down."

"You've got it, sweetheart! If you miss the son of a bitch going up, you can get him coming back down. Just remember, you are hot until you run through the clip. Don't worry about saving ammo. We'll want results no matter how much we have to shoot to get it. Your turn. Shoot at the red boat. It's a perfect target."

"Those guys are on the boat. I don't want to shoot them."

"Honey, those guys are dead. If you end up having to defend us against the gang they were fighting, that gang would be happy to lend these guys as targets. So fire away."

"Jeez, here goes." She pulled the gun into her hip and depressed the trigger. Nothing happened. "What the hell!" she exclaimed.

"You left out a step. A critical one. But in fact, just doing that much is often enough to stop aggressive action. When you are facing down these operatives, though, and you jack a shell into the chamber, they know you are hot. Most of them will stand down, especially when you've got the drop on 'em."

"So I've got to pull this thingy back. Is that it?"

"Yeah, but hammer it back. That puts the first round in the chamber. From there on this thing fires, I don't know, maybe a hundred rounds a minute. It spits the empties out just as fast. Give it a try."

She did and found it gave her the thrilling sense of power. She worked over the red boat, sawing it up and down. When she ran through the clip, she laughed. "That was fun! I want to do it again."

Alec handed her a fresh clip. She ripped the old one out and handed it to him. He tossed it into the river. She slammed her new clip into the receiver, set the sub on her hip, hammered the cocking arm, and touched off a short burst at the boat. She finished the clip, practicing using short bursts and reveling in the sense of formidable power that she felt. "Goddamn, I love this!" she exulted. "Let's just see you throw me into a whorehouse now!"

He laughed with her, thrilling in the firepower they now possessed and the comfort of having her companionship in a brand-new and somewhat frightening perspective. "Are you done?"

"Yeah, I guess we better save the rest of our ammo. But if we have any left when we get to safety, I've got dibs on shooting off what's left."

"You got it," he said. "Now let's load up and get out of here."

Soon after, the twelve-footer was skimming around the downstream bend of the river. Alec showed no concern for fuel consumption and kept up a pressing speed for the next hour. Jordanne wondered what he had in mind. It seemed that they were charging pell-mell into trouble. Anxiously, she looked back at him and shrugged. It was impossible to talk over the drone of the engine. He finally dropped their speed down and kicked the boat into neutral with the throttle at idle. "What are we doing?" She wanted to know.

"Not sure, but we needed to get the hell clear of that disaster. We need to think this thing out."

"You said there would be more of those guys coming up to see what happened to their pals. Shouldn't we be getting out of the middle of the river?"

"Yeah, I think so too. Let's motor back over and look along the north side for a place to hide." Finding a hidey hole proved to be as frustrating as before, dodging mud bars and shallow water. Alec raised the outboard up to the first notch and carefully idled along the shoreline. At length, she pointed to a small stream pouring quietly from a tree stand that resembled mangrove. There was a channel large enough to slip the boat into. They motored upstream, hoping for a place to tuck into. After passing two possibles, they reversed course and looked over what they had bypassed, finally settling on the first. There was no danger of being seen from the river, but the tiny clearing at the water's edge was barely adequate to step out of the boat and spread the tarp for a bed.

"Tonight is hip hole night," he announced.

"What's that?" Jordanne asked suspiciously. "Some kind of new sexual move you dreamed up?"

"You've never hip holed?"

"Never."

"Well, you won't like it much," he said.

Despite the inadequacy of the site, they made the best of it. He showed her how to hollow out a depression in the ground for her hip. Then they spent the rest of the afternoon watching the river. As he had expected, boats came flying from somewhere downstream headed up toward the S bend of the river.

"What are they going to do when they see what happened?" she asked.

"I think they will gather their dead and call it a Mexican stand-off for right now. The man-to-man stuff wasn't healthy for either side. Their next action will probably be ambushes. One on ones and sniping."

"Is that good for us?"

"I wish I knew, sweetheart. I truly wish I knew."

They choffed down the same meal as the night before without the extra festivities and turned in for a night that seemed to last for three days. They started early the next morning. As light intensified on the river, a kaleidoscopic sunrise treated their sleep-bleary eyes. Jordanne gazed at the blended light as it shifted and streamed through the seams of the hills and varying heights of the jungle canopy. "If that were ice cream, what would you call it?"

He looked at the spread of colors for a moment. "Roy G Biv Lime."

"What? Why would you call it that?"

"That's the full panorama of the colors of the rainbow, or the bending of light, plus lime for the jungle."

"What the hell? How do you get the colors of the rainbow out of that?"

"Well, it's red, orange, yellow, green, blue, indigo, and violet. What would you call it?"

"I'd name it for us. SERE Gold."

"Okay. Explain."

"Survive, evade, resist, escape gold."

"You left out a piece."

"What is that?"

"Love."

She turned and looked back at him. "*Awe*, aren't you sweet. You're right. I should have called it LEERS Gold. Sort of a play on words."

"Yeah, well let's hope like hell we can live long enough to make some of that, whatever we call it. We have fuel for today. I'm going to stretch it. But we must save some to search for a place to fuel up. If we go in strapped and dangerous, we might get away with a tankful at one of the marinas. I hope you like using your gat for real like you did shooting up that boat."

"I know. It's life or death, right?"

"Not trying to overdramatize it. But hell yes, it is. I hope we can avoid that. Maybe 'avoid' should be in your ice cream too."

Alec motored on the north side of the river all morning. At half throttle and six hours, he figured he had knocked out seventy miles. That left fifty miles, he thought, but he was only guessing. The braided channels began some fifteen miles from the coast, and that was the start of tide effect, which caused reverse flows in the river.

The fuel level, however, was down to about a half-gallon. They have had to evade discovery by the cartel patrols, which they had discovered pouring out of a marina on the opposite side of the river. As soon as they spotted the first boats, Alec cut the motor, and they spread the tarp over the boat. That had worked. After an hour, he started the motor. Prowling time was upon them. He motored at idle, and they crept along the shore. He had decided to hit the marina across the river the next day after the patrols set out upriver, so his objective was to find a hideout soon, spend the night, and save the fuel he had to reach the marina and to escape if their bluff was called.

He was about to reverse and look at a different angle for a spot, when Jordanne said, "What's that up there?" She pointed to a spot just downstream, where a slow-moving stream eased out of the jungle and into the river. Slack water marked the entry. There appeared to be a small aluminum boat stuck in some soupy mud near the bank, abandoned. An ancient Johnson five-horse motor fully extended with its prop and skeg buried in the mud kept the boat from floating away. There didn't appear to be anyone around.

Alec eagerly steered toward the boat, thinking to scarf the boat's fuel tank. Moving very slowly, he stood up and looked around for the boat's owner. He didn't see the man on the opposite side of the little boat lying face down, half on the bank and half in the water. He was dead. Jordanne was also standing. Both scanned the area, looking for someone, anyone. "What's that smell?" she asked.

"Something's dead," he said. He had no sooner spoken than he felt the first shock coming up from the bottom of the boat through his boots. "Oh shit!" he yelled. "Jordanne! Do not sit down! Do not touch metal! Steady yourself with the wind screen."

"Alec, I'm getting shocked!" She began screaming and capering around, throwing her arms crazily and lifting her legs in a stationary high-stepping dance. When he kicked the boat into reverse, he was hit and nearly knocked out. He grabbed the throttle handle and cranked it carefully to avoid throwing Jordanne down onto the seat. The rubber grip saved him from another jolt. Her screams were continuing but were getting weaker, and she was beginning to fail in her frantic gyrations. The boat backed steadily away from the slack water. In a few moments, Alec cranked the throttle completely and shot the boat to safety. By then, Jordanne had collapsed. He kicked the boat out of gear, killed the motor, and scrambled forward. She lay unconscious and huddled in a heap. He pulled her up and found she was completely limp. He stretched her out on the seat bench and began to give her mouth-to-mouth resuscitation and CPR. It was a minute before she took her first breath. He continued with chest compressions but let her breathe on her own. He checked her pulse every minute by pressing his index finger to a carotid artery in her neck. A couple of minutes later, her pulse was weak but steady. He decided to monitor her for a while without the chest compressions. In about ten minutes, her eyes fluttered open, and she tried to sit up.

He knelt beside her and pressed her back down. "Not just yet, sweetheart. Let's give it a few more minutes."

"What happened?" she said weakly.

"Electric eels."

"They can do that?"

"Those damned things! Each one can generate over five hundred volts. That's five times the shock you can get from the wiring in your apartment. I don't know how many were discharging against the boat. Probably two or three. I got hammered when I hit the reverse lever. The whole boat was electrified. That's why you went down. That smell? That was the guy with the boat. I saw him when we backed away. He had run into them and jumped out when the juice hit him. He didn't quite make it. He was on the bank, half in the water. Dead."

"That's what happened to me?"

"That's what happened to you. Up front, the eels were directly under you. I got us out of there as fast as I could, but you went down. When I got to you, you weren't breathing and had no pulse. I got you back, but you need to rest right now."

"What are we going to do about the eels?"

"Tomorrow, after the cartel boats leave the marina, I'm going to shoot those eels out of there. I want that guy's gas tank. You wanna join me?"

"I've never wanted to kill something this much in my life!"

Alec made her lie down while he cruised back up the shoreline. A mile or so later, he found a gap in the forest, where a creek came into the river at an angle that had hidden it from them when they were motoring downstream. He eased slowly up the small tributary and found it opened into a small pond. As he ran the boat up on the bank, a half dozen turtles scrambled away and dove into the water. He killed and lifted the motor and let the boat settle before stepping across Jordanne to grab the anchor and heave it up on shore. He jerked the boat forward and planted the anchor. When he returned to the boat, she was sitting up, rubbing her arms up and down. "How do you feel?" he asked.

"Forgetful," she said. "Sort of disoriented. Weak. Hateful. I'm wondering 'Why me?' all the time. Alec, you've got to get me out of here! I can't take anymore!" She began sobbing.

"I know," he said. "We're close, babe. We're close. Come on. Let's get you out of the boat, and you can watch the turtles while I set up camp. Tomorrow, we should make El San Sabo."

Camp that night was one of boiling water and turtle stew. Alec had caught a female digging a nesting hole and scooped her off the ground. While he held the struggling amphibian with its legs out and head thrust forward, Jordanne lopped off its head with the machete. He had then pried the body free of the shell. It was loaded with eggs. The meat and eggs, the last of their rice, and two potatoes, boiled with a copious amount of salt, was one of the best feeds they had had on the river.

Jordanne, still recovering from her shock, was the recipient of all the tender attention he could muster, but her mood had turned darker. She was more reticent and not as enthusiastic in her conversation. Alec worried for her and finally asked, "Are you going to be all right?"

She looked at him strangely. "I am all right. I am just through with all this bullshit. Running scared. Worried about the cartels. Worried about being thrown into a whorehouse. Hassled by every son of a bitch looking to rob us. No food. No gas. No water. Sleeping on the ground. Being kidnapped. Being bound till my tits burst. Pretending to be a man. Just being scared shitless all the time. I'm through with it, Alec. I died already. I didn't mind it, and I won't mind it next time. I just don't want to do it here. I don't want this country to be the one to do me in, but if it does, it does. I want out of here as directly as possible. We need gas. That marina has gas. We have that wad of money. We have guns. So in the morning, let's go over there and gas up."

"Okay," he said, "that's a plan."

Chapter 11

Well fed, they waited out the following morning until the armada of armed boats left the marina. When Alec figured the coast was clear, they motored across the river. The weather was clear, bright, and sunny. Jordanne sat up front with one of the AR's loaded, with a full clip resting beside her. Alec motored around the end of a small protective jetty and into the cup of an expansive backwater that formed the marina basin. A village spread out, protected by the bank of the river and the jetty. It looked prosperous. People were busy with the commerce of living and could be seen walking, laughing, and talking in convivial and friendly fashion. The docks were on the side of the marina next to the village. There were two gangways leading up into the village. Small fishing boats were pulled up on the shore to either side of the docks, which were obviously reserved for the needs of the cartel.

Alec began looking for the gas dock. It was stationed away from the regular docks and out in the open water of the marina. It was accessible from both sides, although one gas pump serviced both sides. He had discussed with Jordanne how they were going to approach. She had a rope tied into a cleat near the bend of the bow. He had another tied to the rear cleat, both on the starboard side. She would remain in the boat after they tied up to the dock. He would set their gas tank on the dock and deal with the attendant. She would stand with the AR held loosely at port arms. He would flash the big wad of pesos, clearly willing to overpay for fuel. They hoped that threat and bribery would get them in and out quickly.

Tying up was quickly accomplished. Alec set the tank on the dock and clambered up to stand beside it. He had expected to confront an attendant who didn't speak English, but there was no attendant. He looked into the hut that covered most of the dock and saw a line of eight or nine outboard motor tanks. He stepped inside and quickly checked them out. He found one that was full, with the residue of oil spread out around the filler cap. He figured the residue indicated mixed fuel for two stroke engines, so he picked the tank up and carried it to the edge of the dock by their boat. "Got one," he said to Jordanne. Then he took the near empty, set it in the center of the doorway into the hut, and stuffed three one-hundred-thousand-peso notes under the handle and turned back to their boat.

He had just heaved the full tank into the bottom of the boat and was attaching the fuel line when he heard a booming voice yell from a small boat shooting across from the village side toward them.

"What the living hell do you think you are doing?" bellowed a short fat redheaded Anglo through a full badly matted beard. He pulled his boat up to a short set of steps at the end of the dock, quickly tied off a bow line, and stepped smoothly onto the dock. He came charging around the side of the hut, pulling a sidearm from a holster snugged high against his right hip. He wore a blue-and-orange flowered Hawaiian shirt, loose over a baggy pair of dirty white shorts. His gut flopped over the shorts and bulged the shirt. He was barefoot. "This is a private dock!" he thundered. "You can't just barge in here and help yourself," he continued, bringing his handgun to bear in Alec's direction.

"Oh, I wouldn't do that if I were you," Alec said mildly.

"Oh, you wouldn't, would cha."

"Jordanne?"

"Got him."

The redhead noticed her for the first time. "Hell, she's just a woman! Women don't have the guts to shoot a man in cold blood."

She jerked the cocking arm of the sub back into its firing position and leveled the gun straight at the blustering man. "This one does," she said with a cold detachment that frightened the man into a cowering position, turning himself away from the rock steady bore of the machine gun.

"Hey, lady! No offense. Point that thing somewhere else, please!"

"Holster your sidearm," Alec suggested quietly. "She will keep you covered, but as long as you don't do something stupid, she probably won't shoot."

"What do you mean, probably won't?" he asked nervously, stuffing his nine back into its holster.

"After what she's been through, she just doesn't give a shit anymore."

"Well, Jesus Christ, man!" the fellow pleaded. "Can't you tell her to point that thing up or down or off to the side?"

"'Fraid not. She's like those cobras over there in Africa. They just rear up and never stop looking right at you. And she's on her own here. You try to bullshit us, and your guts have a 90 percent chance of being hung on this dock. Now let's do some business. My empty can is sitting right there where you can see it. You will notice payment for the replacement fuel is stuffed into the handle. There is a very handsome tip included for you as well."

The redhead looked at the can, recognizing the color of the bills stuffed inside the handle. "Sweet Jesus," he muttered. "Yeah, yeah sure, we can do some business. Is that all you want?"

"I also need some information. I'll pay for it as long as it's honest. The lady back there will watch and listen. She has a bullshit detector you won't believe. Oh, wait! You won't have a chance to live long enough to believe it. Sorry about that, old chap. My bad. What I need to know is how far is it to El San Sabo?"

"Sixty-five miles, but if you've never been there, you probably won't know which channel to take. Getting lost in the channels is easy to do."

Alec grinned at the man. "My name is Alec. That's Jordanne. What do you call yourself?"

"It used to be Bill, but right now it's Willy."

"Well, Willy, this is your lucky day! For a very handsome reward, you are going to volunteer to guide us to yon fair city."

"I can't do that!" he cried. "I've got to refuel the cartel boats when they get back and check 'em for oil. Clean 'em up for tomorrow. Those guys will kill me if I'm not here when they get back."

"Willy, if you aren't here, they can't kill you, but we are here, and if you don't step into this boat, your worries about the cartel won't matter. Now, when we safely get to El San Sabo, you are going to help us get situated to fly out of there. You, too, will be able to fly out safe and sound and well set up to start your life in some meaningful way somewhere else. Or you can hatch up some cock-and-bull story for the cartel and come back here. I don't care. But right now, you have a quick decision to make. We aren't leaving a witness who can go bellowing like a bell cow spreading the alarm. Get it, Willy?"

The man looked at Jordanne, standing insolently at the bow of the boat as she stared at him. The barrel of her machine gun was still rock steady and zeroed on his gut. "Okay, I'm going with you," he said, starting to step into the boat.

"Hold it, Willy," Alec said sharply, pointing at the fuel can in the hut. "That's your money."

"Oh yeah, so scared I forgot."

They left quietly. Willy sat up front, unarmed, with Jordanne sitting behind him with her submachine gun held in her lap with the barrel pointed off him but at an angle where she could instantly bring it into play. Alec sat beside her on the port side, running the boat. He swung around the point of the jetty and hit full throttle. Even with Willy's additional 220 pounds, the boat came up on plane, and soon, they were skimming along at an admirable twenty-two miles an hour. Alec held into center of the current for an hour and a half at full throttle. It was then that Willy held his hands up over his head. Alec slowed down to idle to see what he wanted and so they could each other talk. "What do you want, Willy?" Alec asked.

Willy popped a leg over, straddling the seat. "With this much weight in this boat, running it full out with a fifteen-horse motor, we won't make it to San Sabo. You've got to cut back to half throttle. Just up on plane. Even then, with what you've gone through, we might have to be towed in, but getting a tow won't be hard."

Then he stood up and yelled, "Oh no! Oh fuck! Here they come!"

Alec looked over his shoulder and saw a speedboat a mile or so behind them coming hard. "Willy, who's 'they'?"

"The cartel. A boat must have come back early. They checked with one of their informants who told them I was in this boat heading downriver. We're fucked!"

"Not without a fight, we aren't. Sit down, Willy! Jordanne, straddle the center seat and get ready."

With that, he twisted the throttle and wiggled the boat up on plane and sped downriver as he glanced backward. The speed boat had closed the gap, and a sturdy Colombian, who had a pair of binoculars strapped around his neck, braced his legs against the port side of the boat amidships and raised an automatic to his shoulder. "Coming about," Alec hollered as he slammed the control arm to the right as hard as it would go. The boat spun hard to port as the speedboat shot by. The shooter touched off a burst, and there was the tinny sound of bullets pinging the bow in front of the wind screen. "I need a gun! I need a gun!" Willy howled, looking about him frantically.

"Under the bow!" Jordanne screamed. "Other side of that backpack!"

Willy jerked down and plowed into the pile on the opposite side of the dividing panel and popped back up with one of the other guns in his hands. "We've got a chance, now!" he squealed. "I'm a good shot!"

Alec had the boat running back upriver. Guessing the speedboat would turn to port to match the direction of his turn, he yelled, "Coming about to the left! You guys swing around!" Both Willy and Jordanne spun on their respective bench seats. As the cartel boat came speeding back at them on their port side, Willy opened up and proved his worth. His lead stitched the water and climbed the side of the cartel boat, taking out the gunner, even as the shooter's own burst cut a springing line of punctures through their boat between Willy and Jordanne. As the blue and white of the slick boat shot by, Jordanne turned and fired a long burst at the back of the driver of the receding boat. Alec ducked hard right as she fired over his shoulder. Suddenly, there was a blossom of red in the center of the driver's back, and the boat shot hard a port and began turning a tight circle ever slowing until it stopped.

"We're taking on water!" Willy yelled. "Head for the cartel boat!"

Alec turned to starboard and hammered back downstream. There were six inches of water sloshing about in the bottom of the boat, with spurts of water arcing in as Alec pulled up alongside the stern ladder of the blue-and-white boat that was idling and turning a quiet circle in the middle of the river. Willy scrambled aboard and hit the kill switch. Then he rooted about in a side compartment and came out with a sealed tube. "You got a knife?" he called to Alec. Alec tossed him his clasp knife. "Get your stuff thrown on board," he ordered. Then he cut off the tip of the tube and leaned over the side of the cartel boat and began squeezing caulk into the bullet holes on the port side, where his burst had crawled up and into the shooter who now slumped down, dead and bleeding out.

Alec and Jordanne were loading their stuff into the speed boat. The rifle, handguns, machine guns, ammo bags, machete, backpack, tarp and net, and fish stunner made quite a pile. Willy, having finished caulking bullet holes, looked back as he pulled the driver over to the side next to the shooter. "Jesus! You two don't exactly travel light, do you?" he exclaimed. Then suddenly, he added, "Oh my god! You two are the ones started that goldrush up on the Rio Estrella! I'll be goddamned! You are famous. But everyone figured you for dead! You just disappeared when everybody was looking for you. Wow! I am a lucky son of a bitch. You don't need to point that gun at me anymore, Jordanne," he finished happily. "Now, I'm one of us!"

"All right, Willy," Alec said, "welcome to hell. You are in for some serious shit. Now what do we do with those two?"

"That's easy, there's a hell of a concentration of man-eating caiman downstream a few miles. We'll dump 'em there, clean up the boat, and run on into San Sabo. I know guys in a marina there who can give us a hand. It'll cost but when they're paid, they're good."

"What about the little boat?"

"What about it?"

"Shouldn't we tow it over to the side, out of the main current?"

"Hell no! Maybe a cartel boat will hit it and take out their outdrive. We don't have time to fart around with it. We've got to go. Sit down and grab something. We'll be doing seventy-five in two minutes." He turned to Jordanne, "Grab a seat, beautiful, and hang on to that gat. You just might need it again."

He fired up the engine, hit the bilge pump, and waited until it pissed the water the boat had taken on from bullet holes. Jordanne asked him why he didn't plug the bullet holes she had punched into the stern. "Those won't go through the transom. Too thick," he grinned. "Makes shooting out the back a lot safer than standing up, like that fool I shot was doing. No, we're good for leaks. That caulk I used is special stuff. Seals right now, dries flexible. You can paint right over it too. Yeah. Real good stuff. Okay, boys and girls, let's have some fun!"

With that, Willy punched the throttle lever forward. The boat hit plane, and he trimmed it out. In seconds, it seemed like they were going into lift off. He knew exactly which channel to take, and he never let off the throttle. It didn't matter which way the current flowed, the boat was designed and built for speed. It seemed to skate atop the water, and Willy knew how to keep it from cavitating or pounding into the wakes of other boats or waves generated by wind. Alec and Jordanne kept their heads down. About ten minutes later, Willy dropped it down and cut toward the south side of the river. "Here we are," he said. "Give me a hand with these two." Alec moved forward, and after Willy searched the pockets of each, they flopped the two over the side. There was a rush as caiman shot out of the shallows and jerked the corpses under. "Hey, I got a couple hundred bucks worth off those guys. You want some?" he asked Alec.

"No thanks, I'm good."

"How about you?" he queried Jordanne. She shook her head. "Okay, your loss." He backed out of the caiman den and cut the motor. "We'll take a few minutes to clean her up," he continued. His rummaging in the boat was on point. He knew where everything was. He came up with a towel, and a spray bottle of cleanser of some kind. "You wouldn't believe the number of blood spots I've scrubbed out of these boats over the past five years," he said. In a few minutes, he stood up, satisfied. "That'll do," he said. "Hopefully, the next blood spot won't be one of ours."

"How far back there are they?"

"Oh, don't worry about them. They won't have time to catch up. They'll radio ahead. It's the ones ahead of us we've got to crack. I noticed three subs. One for each of us. Let's get locked and loaded right now. Here's how they do this. Four boats across the river. Two broadside, two flankers—stern to. They want to be able to chase immediately if the target boat gets by. Most targets slow down to assess and maybe turn back. We won't. You guys need to be up front. You're going to shoot down the port side and up the center. I've got the starboard. I'm going to split the broadside pair. Going to be a hell of a jolt. We're not going straight in. We're zigzagging. Don't stand up. If you do, you'll go over. That happens, it's Sayonara, been nice knowin' ya. They're gonna have us out manned and out gunned. What we have on our side is the speed of our attack, an unpredictable method of attack, and shooting first. Shoot when you hear me open up. They will have two shooters in each broadside boat, and two in the sterns of each of the other two boats. Eight altogether. Remember, when I shoot, open up from inside out. You won't have time to rake 'em more than once. If we can take out a couple of them, fine. What we really want is to make them duck. So shoot straight. We don't have time to waste with a question-and-answer session. Last thing, when we split the two center boats drop to the floor and grab a piece of the deck. And don't stand up! All right, kids, here we go! San Sabo in twenty minutes or so, if we get lucky."

Willy soon had them underway and driving downriver at seventy-five miles an hour. Alec put Joranne on the port side of the bow. "You'll have to shoot left-handed," he hollered into her ear, "but you'll have some cover. Finish your clip whatever you do! When we hit the deck, we'll grab each other."

"Got it!" she yelled back. They looked at each other deeply before turning to look downriver for the blockade.

Willy kept the boat on an unerring course through channels that led off in a dozen different angles. He never looked to the sides. With his head tucked beneath the plexiglass wind screen, he was focused on what he was going to do. Alec and Jordanne kept their heads down to keep their eyes from blurring out. Time flew for Willy and crawled for the lovers. It all came to a head in less than a half hour.

Willy spotted the blockade, laid out just as he had described it. He leaned down so his voice could be heard. "Game time!" he shouted. The two popped up and glanced against the wind quickly before ducking back down out of the blast. It was just as Willy had described it would be. They waited anxiously for him to start shooting. Then he maxed out the boat, and it jumped to an even greater speed. The boat also began zipping from side to side. It was a sickening force that pitched them from side to side without rhythm. Willy suddenly bellowed," Get ready!" The boat straightened out and ran evenly. Alec rose up and braced himself, keeping his head ducked.

Willy opened up. He swept from left to right. Alec focused on the center and made sure he finished the clip. Jordanne simply worked over the boat on the left. She remembered to empty her clip. There was a wild hail of lead sailing by them, but it was the result of men diving for cover, and it sailed high and wide. Willy dropped his head and bellowed sideways at them. "Grab your asses!" They dove for each other and rolled together just as there was a tremendous impact that caused their boat to lift and sail forward online between the two blocking boats. Debris ripped by at a hellacious rate. They were jammed forward but clung tightly together as the boat banged back down to the water, skipped, and steadied out.

Willy dropped the speed gradually until they could see what had happened behind them. His greatest fear was the two chase boats. Each one, however, had been taken out by a blocking boat that had been spun, driven up, against and over them. With the chase boats taken out, Willy cut power, and they took inventory of the damage to their boat. The forward deck and hull on the port side had split and caved in. On the starboard side, the force of the impact had crumpled the bow, but the deck and hull still held together. As such, their wreck was still afloat. They were forced to motor at a comparative snail's pace not to draw attention, although the condition of the boat was bad enough that they were noticed anyway. Willy drove fast enough to keep the bow up out of the water.

Alec wanted to know how much longer it would take to make the harbor. "Oh, we won't go in there," said Willy. "Cartels will have that battened down tighter than a bull's ass. We're going to see one of my guys. Meantime, you two could reload and cover our ass. I don't think they can recover, and if they do, they will probably head into the marina. It's an outside shot, but they might come this way. Let's not get caught with our panties around our ankles."

Roughly a tense half hour later, they motored into a secluded duck-in hole in the dense jungle on the south side at the mouth of the river. The small bay contained a dock that jutted out from the shore into the water, some thirty feet. A ramshackle building with a tin roof was built back against the heavy overweening canopy that was almost an umbrella. Beside the shack was also a building that was obviously a shop. It was clad in rusting metal that gave it an air of near abandonment. Willy tossed lines that he pulled from storage compartments on either side of the boat. Alec stepped onto the dock and helped tie the boat off to dock cleats. Jordanne was getting set to heave their stuff onto the dock. Willy looked at the pile and made a suggestion. "The only thing I see there that you are going to need is that backpack. The last thing the two of you are going to want to do is to be caught in San Sabo strapped. The rest of it, you are through with. You're out of one jungle, but now you are into another. My guys and I are going to have your backs."

Alec leaned down and said, "Well, you heard our partner, my dear, hand me the backpack and step up on the dock."

"Yes, master," she said. "Is this my whorehouse?"

"What?" Willy blurted, completely confounded.

Alec clapped him on the shoulder. "Private joke, my friend, private joke. Are we supposed to do something here besides stand on the dock?"

"Come on," Willy said, "let's go meet my guy, Art."

Art was watching them from the doorway of the shack. He was drawn back in the shadow of a darkened entryway. Willy walked up and right in. Art stepped aside. Alec and Jordanne stopped. Art smiled. "Come on in," he said. Inside, the room was neat and clean. There was nothing personal to distinguish it. The walls were bare.

It was sparsely furnished with a small love seat and three straight backed chairs. A small kitchenette was built into one corner of the room. It was apparently used for coffee only. Art invited them to sit. Alec and Jordanne took the love seat. "Today, I'm Art Lebo," the man said by way of introduction.

"Alec Jones, Jordanne Austin." Neither man offered to shake hands.

Art asked if anyone wanted coffee. "Fresh pot," he said. Alec and Jordanne looked at each other. They nodded quickly at the same time. Art rose, he was tall, well over six feet, and built like an athlete. He was bald, well-tanned, and tattooed extensively. He appeared to be fifty or so years old. He was graceful in his movements and obviously efficient at whatever he set out to do. He didn't ask if they wanted cream or sugar. The cups he brought to them were oversized and clean. The coffee was hot and only moderately strong. That the two of them were overwhelmed was obvious.

"My god," Jordanne spoke softly, "I forgot how wonderful a simple cup of coffee can be. Thank you."

Alec sipped and nodded. "Damned good. Thanks."

They sat for a few moments while Alec and Jordanne enjoyed their coffee. Then Art turned to Willy. "So what have we got here?"

"These are the two that started the gold rush."

Art abruptly stood up. "You've got to be shitting me! How did you capture them?"

"Other way around." Willy grinned. He briefly told Art what had happened at the gas dock.

Art laughed delightedly. He looked at Alec and Jordanne. "I am pleased to meet you two. Your story has been told up and down this river for weeks. The big cartels have even been interested in you two. That's hard to scare up. The smaller gangs have heard that you are carrying millions in gold. That's why they wanted your asses. That and one of the most ravishing blondes been on the river, in like, forever. Double haul worth millions and millions! You two started two goldrushes is what you did."

Willy stepped into Art's comments, "I didn't tell her why she was the second gold rush, Art."

Jordanne smiled. "Don't be concerned. He did." She elbowed Alec, who turned away struggling not to spill his coffee.

"Had to keep her focused," he said.

"So, Willy, how come you to have a beat-up cartel boat?"

"We were running in a twelve-footer, with a fifteen-horse kicker pushing. One of the patrol boats came back early. Got the story of me being kidnapped and came after us, guns hot. We won."

"And you ran the blockade. Usual setup?"

"Yep, two across, two pursuits."

"How did you bust it?"

"Came in zigzag, redlined, guns hot, split the center. Got lucky."

"What do I need to do?"

"Got to get rid of the boat. I need cover to leave for the states. Passport, documents. Flight to Cancun with connections to Miami. New name and ID."

"How about these two?"

"They're gonna contact the consulate. They're legit. They'll need protection, though, ID and docs to leave the country. Same thing I'm doing. Fly to Cancun and to wherever from there."

"And this is being paid for, how?"

"You get the boat. Some handguns, a rifle, three subs. Some cash or gold, I'm guessing, from them."

"What's the story with the gold?"

Willy looked at Alec and shrugged. "Have to ask them?"

"Willy, is Art compromised?" Alec immediately asked.

"Holy shit! Don't ask me that!" Willy exclaimed in alarm.

"You are in this thing with us, aren't you?"

"Yeah, but Jesus! Art, I'm sorry!"

Art stared evenly at Alec. "Why the question?"

"Because I need help from people who aren't cartel threatened. I don't know you. Willy does. After what happened today, he has no safe harbor here at all. He is, as he just stated, going to have to fly out as well. Maybe with us. If he trusts you, then so do I."

"Alec," Willy said, "I trust Art completely."

"Good enough. Here's the story of the gold. Up at the head of the Rio Estrella, you can walk along gravel bars and kick nuggets the size of the end of your thumb out with your foot. She did it two or three times while I panned. This is what we have left." Alec opened the backpack, reached to the bottom, and pulled out the shirt sleeve pouch with a grunt. "It isn't millions and millions. It was all I could do to haul that out."

"Mind if I take a look?" Art asked.

"Not at all. Willy has my knife. He can cut the string."

"Oh, hell, I forgot to give it back. Alec, sorry."

He cut the binding at the top, closed and returned the knife. Art opened the pouch and said, "Very nice. How long did it take you to fill this thing?"

"I panned three times. Total of maybe ten hours."

"Mind if I weigh it?"

"I'd be delighted."

Art went to a cupboard beside the kitchenette. He pulled out a large scoop-shaped pan and a digital scale. He handed the scale to Willy and the pan to Alec. "Hang onto these for a second," he said. Then from the wall behind the door, he pulled out a small folding table, which he sat up in the middle of the room. He took the scale, calibrated it with the pan set on the flat plate on the top of the scale. "Okay, kids, this thing reads in ounces so, little lady, why don't you call out the numbers by the hundred."

He started the pour, and she counted to five. He turned the sleeve inside out and shook the last flakes into the pan. The final weight was 564.7 ounces.

"That's thirty-five pounds. No wonder you grunted and groaned packing that along with everything else in that pack," he said, looking at Alec with admiration.

"So how much is that worth?" Jordanne asked.

"Well," he said, holding his watch up level and punching in some numbers, "we reduce the sixteen-ounce count to twelve Troy ounces. Costs you 18 percent on the conversion. That's 463 Troy ounces. Gold closed in New York yesterday at 1865. You are looking at $863,595.71."

Jordanne looked at Alec. "What are we going to do?"

He looked at Art and Willy. "Being a complete novice at this, is there some way you fellas know of to get this stuff out of country?"

They both laughed. Willy, chortling, said, "You're in Colombia, Mack! Smuggling is a way of life here. Of course, we know ways. Hell, I been workin' for a cartel for five years!"

Art smiled at Jordanne. "Just tell us where you want it delivered."

Alec looked at her. She stared back. "Can we tell you tomorrow?" she asked.

"Sure, take as long as you want."

"Let's do it this way," Alec said. "Willy, where are you headed?"

"Somewhere in Florida to start."

"Okay. You take it. We'll give you contact information, and you can get in touch with us when you get squared away."

"Are you sure? There will be some expenses. You will have to approve them."

"Willy, you are one of us. We're partners that have faith in one another. You take care of Art and whoever else and whatever else. That's your end of the deal. Ours was getting the gold down here. Just do your best, that's all."

"Is it okay to pay in gold?"

"Isn't that the best way to fly?"

"I like the way you think. It certainly is."

With Willy handling the gold, that freed Alec and Jordanne to keep the cash they had gotten from Father Sebastian. Alec didn't know how much was left. He would check that later. For the moment, they were going to inspect the boat.

Art looked at the boat for structural damage from both inside and out. He crawled out of the interior and stepped up on the dock. "It's doable," he said. "Let's get her on the track and into the shed."

Alec and Jordanne sat on the dock while Art and Willy moved the boat onto a double rail and winch setup that pulled the blue boat through a double set of doors in the side of the shed. Power for the operation of the winch was provided by a gas-powered generator that Art had fired up when they had the winch line attached to the boat. Inside fifteen minutes the boat was locked down, its cartel life over.

After repairs, its new life would begin in a country to the south. Said country to be named later.

The two men walked back to the dock. "Let's go have another cup of coffee," Art offered. "Your taxi won't be here for another half hour or so." They all trooped back to the shack. Art brewed fresh coffee, and when they were all seated, he asked, "How come you two were up the Rio Estrella?"

Alec related the story of the crash. "I kept expecting some kind of search would be made, but there was nothing even though the pilot did all the location stuff. So we hiked out. The rest of the story is one nightmare after another, although I did build one hell of a raft, if I do say so, myself."

"I'm guessing," Art commented, "that your plane went down during the attempted coup on the government awhile back. Probably put the civilian air patrol, such as it is, on hold. They don't lose, so much as throw out stuff like lost airplane reports whenever that happens."

"It wasn't all a nightmare," Jordanne piped up, "I was a goddess!"

Art looked at her and smiled. "Even now you qualify, but how did that occur back up there in the jungle?"

She explained the event, and when she was through, Art confirmed what Alec had told her about the voodoo beliefs of some native tribes. "So how's your back?" Art asked Alec.

"She's been straightening it pretty much ever since," he deadpanned. Willy and Art looked away trying to stifle silly grins.

Jordanne looked at all three men, trying to understand their mirth. "No, I haven't. That medicine man putting the poultices on your ass is what got your back straightened out. I didn't do anything."

The men broke out in laughter. "What's so damned funny?" She wanted to know.

Alec finally told her, "It's an old, old expression men use. I'll explain it to you later."

"You better, or you'll be sorry," she retorted.

The drone of a motor ended the conversation. "Here's your taxi," Art said. "Let's go see what accommodations you are getting?"

"Accommodations?" Alec asked, puzzled. "How did that happen? I thought we would be doing that ourselves."

"Do you want to find yourselves back upriver again?"

"No. That's off my bucket list for damn sure."

"Then you need to follow any and all instructions you get from us until you get back to the States. Don't think for a minute that you can be involved in killing members of any of these big cartels down here and just start waltzing around as though nothing happened. When you get home, you'd be well advised to invest in security as well. The tentacles of the cartels reach around the world."

Jordanne looked at Alec, tears forming in her eyes. "Is this ever going to end?"

He looked grim as he replied, "That's out of our hands, I guess."

They walked down to the dock where an eighteen-foot tri-hull I/O was idling, waiting for them. Art stopped them while he spoke to the driver. They spoke in fluent Spanish. He turned and smiled. "You're in luck, Mr. and Mrs. Lawrence Adams. You will stop for an hour at a halfway stop, where you will clean up, shave, get a haircut, including you, Jordanne, and get some nice touristy clothes. You will also receive luggage, so get ready to part with your beloved backpack. You will check in at an off the beat hotel. Don't be alarmed at the sound of that. It is quite clean and updated despite its less than savory appearance from the curb. Jordanne, you are now Joanne. Here is your wedding and engagement ring set. Don't fall in the love with the diamond, it's glass."

"So these are our aliases for how long?" Alec asked.

"You will get papers from the consulate in your real names, but until you hit the States, your assumed identities are your safest way to get there. Day after tomorrow, you will get your documents in the names of the Adams. After you get cleaned up and get checked in at your hotel, you will have your pictures taken for your driver's licenses. Until then, you are free to browse, shop, enjoy food, and drink. Men will shadow you. If you notice them, ignore them. Doing otherwise could get you and them shot. Do not contact the consulate until you have your new documents." He added drily, "Keep your new identities secret from the consul. Mustn't have you caught running duplicate IDs, now, must we?"

"Check," Jordanne said, "the tough is going shopping again."

Art looked amused. "I wish I had met you about fifteen years ago. We would have had some times. I am assuming you have cash for shopping?" he added, looking at Alec.

"We do."

"All right. I think it's time to say goodbye."

The men shook hands. Alec told Willy to contact him at Able Mining Consultants in Omaha when the decks were cleared. The Adams boarded the tri-hull and in moments they saw the last of Art Lebo.

Chapter 12

The halfway stop was a bed-and-breakfast facility with the amenities of a hair stylist on call. She was a Colombian native who spoke English. After Alec and Jordanne had showered and brushed their teeth, another simple pleasure they had taken for granted. They both walked into the hair stylist's small studio both wearing bath robes and feeling luxurious. She worked with Jordanne first, calling her Joanne. They looked through a style book and decided on a classic shoulder length with short bangs. Alec watched the transformation of a beauty to one of stunning beauty. He couldn't get over his good fortune. A plan began to form in his mind. When Jordanne's cut was finished, the lady called Mr. Adams to step forward. Alec took a moment to realize he was Adams.

The stylist called him Lawrence as she used scissors to reduce his beard. Then she gave him a shave, followed by a haircut of medium length. He asked how much he owed her, and she said it had been taken care of.

Jordanne was very pleased with the result. "Hello, handsome," she said, taking his arm. "Going my way?"

"I could be," he said. "Were you sent here to save me from the whorehouses?"

"Why yes, I was! I was informed that you are very weak, and I'll be required to work very hard to keep you straightened out. We need to start right away."

So the two returned to their room as a married couple for the first time and worked as she had proscribed.

Later, they counted their money pouch. When converted, they figured they had around a thousand dollars' worth of pesos. Then they showered again and dressed to go to dinner. They found a taxi waiting for them when they emerged from the B&B. Alec asked if there was somewhere they could find steak and potatoes. The driver told them in English, "No problem. When you have finished your dinner, I will be waiting for you."

"We are finding a lot of English-speaking people all of a sudden," Jordanne mentioned to the cab driver.

"Everyone detailed to you will speak English," he replied. "That's so you can respond instantly to commands. Hopefully, you will do so immediately without delay. It's what saves lives."

She looked at Alec as they settled into the back seat of the cab, "I wonder if they are taking odds on us getting outta here alive," she whispered.

"Good question," he said. "They seem to think of everything. Look, even the windows in this cab are tinted too dark for anyone to see into."

As he spoke, a barrier slid up in front of them, sealing the back seat from the front. Subdued lights came on, and a small bar dropped down, stocked with airline-sized bottles of spirits. It also contained small bottles of water and sodas. Plastic cups were also provided. The cabbie's voice came quietly over an intercom system.

"You will have time for a cocktail before dinner if you wish," he said. "I apologize for no ice."

Jordanne whispered again, "There could be film at eleven, so you just keep your hand off my ass, mister!"

"How did you get from 'I want a kid a year' to 'Keep your hand off my ass' all inside a month and a half, or for however many years this nightmare has been going on?"

"I may be a slut, but I am a private one," she said impishly. "I kiss publicly though."

They both had a simple cola and bourbon drink. The car had stopped for some time before the cabbie opened the door. He ushered them quickly into a small café, where all the tables were occupied, except for the one they were escorted to. Menus in English were already placed on the table. "Alec, maybe we should just order takeout," Jordanne said, sotto voice. "No one else in here is eating."

"What was that, Joanne?"

"Sorry, Larry. This whole deal is already creeping me out."

"Lawrence."

"Bullshit. That's a tight-ass pussy's name. Larry is bad enough."

"Jesus, Mrs. Adams, let's just figure out what we are going to eat."

Despite the tight security and lurking danger, the two thoroughly enjoyed their meal. The trip to their hotel was uneventful. The backpack met its demise. They kept nothing from it. Neither were into reminders. Both enjoyed sleeping in a bed for the first time in many weeks. Both fell asleep almost instantly and slept deeply.

Security was tightly maintained the following day as well, even though both Americans were able to stroll through plazas, actually doing some relaxing while shopping. While Jordanne was busy shopping for shoes for a dress she had bought, Alec wandered over to a jewelry display. When he returned to the shoe shop, she had picked out a pair of heels, with four-inch spikes. He approved, thinking they could be eight inchers, and if she liked them, he loved them.

They tired of shopping before lunch. They also tired of just walking around. After a light midday snack, they returned to their hotel. They spent the rest of the day lounging around. Jordanne showered several times. Then she took a bath. She finally lay down on the bed on her back with her bathrobe open. Alec looked up from perusing a newspaper, even though he couldn't understand it. He rose and walked over, sat, and kissed her. "You wanna make a kid, lady?" he asked.

"You can try, but you won't be able to do that," she responded.

"Oh, yeah? What if I give you the hot stuff?"

"Sweetheart," she said, "come here and look at me."

Somewhat confused, he said, "This isn't the brushoff, is it?"

"No. You aren't getting rid of me that easy. I'm telling you, you can't make a kid."

"Why not?"

"Because you already did."

He looked at her as though she were kidding. "How do you know that? Doesn't that mean you have to kill a rabbit first?"

"Oh, I know. Did it ever occur to you that I didn't menstruate in all that time we were mucking around out there?"

"No. I guess I also didn't notice you wanting me to run down to the corner grocery to pick up those things. I just didn't think about that. Jesus, things are really picking up momentum around here."

"What does that mean?"

"Well, you need to stand up. Take off that phony set of rings, please."

"Why, I'm getting to like 'em."

"Nyet!" he said, shaking a finger at her.

She had to wet her finger to slide the rings free. He took them and set them on the nightstand. He reached into his pants pocket and pulled out a small blue box. He opened it and drew out a ring studded with small diamonds. He knelt on one knee before her. "Jordanne Austin," he said, "I love you with all my heart. Will you marry me?"

"Yes, oh god, yes!" She stood trembling as he placed the ring on her finger. Then she started to collapse. He caught her and laid her back on the bed.

Suddenly scared, he asked, "Jordanne, are you all right?"

She reached for him, pulled him to her for a long lingering kiss. "Yes, I'm all right. I've never been this happy in my life. To be yours is all the gold I want from this experience. I love you with all my heart and soul."

That night was the sweetest in all the years of their lives.

The next morning, a courier delivered their Adams' documents. They tucked them into the luggage that had replaced the backpack and called for their private cab. Alec directed the cabbie to take them to the American consulate. After an hour's wait, they were escorted into the office of the head consul. Alec introduced Jordanne to the consul, Andrew Whittaker. He then introduced himself and stated his occupation. Whittaker interrupted. "Don't tell me! You two came down the river from the Rio Estrella, didn't you? An American man and an impossibly beautiful blonde woman. With all due respect, Miss Austin, I now understand why that sentiment was so enthusiastically expressed."

Jordanne blushed and said, "Thank you."

Alec could only say, "Yes, we did come here from the Rio Estrella."

"It's said that you brought out millions of dollars' worth of gold. Is that right?"

"No. We brought out some gold that started the stampede, but it was a small amount. We used it to buy a boat."

"How much is a small amount?"

"I would estimate no more than five or six Troy ounces. A few nuggets. It might have been less. I had no scale."

"Who did you buy the boat from?"

"The transaction was actually a donation to a church that gave us the boat."

"What was the reason you were up there?"

"That is why we are here. We were the only survivors of a plane crash."

Alec went on to explain the consequences of the accident.

Whittaker pulled a file from a drawer. "Do you know the tail numbers of the plane?"

"No."

"Are they still there, by chance?"

Alec looked at Jordanne. "Do you remember any numbers on the fuselage?"

"I don't remember what the numbers were, but there were some numbers, maybe a foot high."

Whittaker nodded. "Is there any way to get back into the crash site?"

"I can show you where it is on a map that shows the Rio Estrella."

"A team will have to go back in to retrieve the bodies for DNA analysis. Would you be available to return to guide a recovery team?"

"No."

"Let me give you some information that might change your mind. That flight, if it can be verified, was insured. The aircraft for one, $.5 million. Each passenger for $1 million. I have a copy of the beneficiary statement. Of interest to you two is that you, Miss Austin, are named as the beneficiary of two who were on the flight. A

Mr. and Mrs. Harry Mangum. That is a two-million-dollar benefit. Tax free, Miss Austin. But it is uncollectible until DNA confirms the identity of the deceased."

"Let me be clear, Mr. Whittaker," Alec said. "Neither my fiancé nor I are going back into that country."

"Without impugning the integrity of my host country, Mr. Jones, the availability of investigative teams is somewhat unreliable. Even when available, they are often not given to reliability. In the event of inconclusive evidence, the insurance company will not pay off. I must go on record as having strongly urged you to take steps to protect your interests."

"Thank you, sir," Alec said. "I assume one could employ independent agents who could represent one's interests couldn't one?"

"Yes. But those agents would of necessity have to be Colombian."

"Thank you for that information. Is there anything else you need from us?"

"No, but please leave your contact information with my secretary. Here is my card in the event you need to speak to me in the future. Miss Austin, it is my pleasure to have met you. I wish both of you the best in concluding this venture. Also, my condolences to you for your loss, Miss Austin."

The Adams returned to their cab. Larry advised the caddie that he had an important message for Willy. The cabbie listened to his request for assistance in aiding an investigation team in retrieving the bodies of an airplane crash in the Rio Estrella. His message finished with: "Just be sure it's kept clean for the insurance company."

The following day, the Adams flew out of Colombia.

Seven months later

Alec and Jordanne had married. They had set up housekeeping in Omaha upon their return to the States. He returned to work with the company for which he had worked for many years. It took five months, but the insurance company had paid the beneficiary benefit to Jordanne. She bought a house, which she claimed was a wedding gift to Alec. He laughed and said that after all the hell she had put him through, it wasn't enough.

One day in the last week of the seventh month, Alec received a strange call from an anonymous caller. He recognized the voice and extended a dinner invitation to its owner. He telephoned Jordanne and told her an old friend of theirs was coming to dinner. Promptly at six o'clock, a dark-haired man rang the doorbell. Alec answered the bell. "Come in, Willy. It's wonderful to see you. I'm glad you called. I wouldn't have recognized you."

Willy laughed. "Had to change a few things. Hair color. Lost fifty pounds. Change of address. It was a hairy trip by the time it all ended, believe me."

Jordanne stepped out of the kitchen and smiled.

Willy looked at Alec. "I thought she was beautiful on the river, but my god, she is beyond anything I ever hoped to see." He teared up, and she embraced him as best she could over a very large abdomen. "You're gonna have a baby!" he said happily.

"Two," she said.

"Oh my god! Twins. When are you due?"

"Well, I started straightening his back on the river about a month before we got out of there. So the best guess is next month."

"So," Willy laughed, "he told you!"

"Yes, he finally did."

During dinner, Willy explained all that had gone on with their gold. "There is in a bank in Florida, $489,264.17, in an account in my name. That's what's left. It took a lot of gold to get the remains off that ridge. I took some of the gold for what I did, so that money in Florida is yours. I just need your banking information to get it to you."

Alec looked at Jordanne. "Shall we?"

She nodded, smiled, and said, "You don't need our banking information, Willy. That part of the gold from the Rio Estrella is yours."

The End.

About the Author

Stevens McClellan is the pen name of Tom Kendall, a sixth-generation Oregonian. He is a retired English and Science teacher whose life experiences include growing up on farms and ranches, working as a lookout and firefighter, railroader, slaughterhouse worker, and finance man. He is a published poet. He lives with his wife, Judy, in Spokane Valley, Washington.